PRAISE FOR
DANIEL LANG'S

CASUALTIES
OF
WAR

"A CLASSIC STATEMENT OF THE
HORRORS OF
THE VIETNAM WAR . . ."
The New Yorker

"*CASUALTIES OF WAR* COULD RESURRECT
ISSUES THAT TRANSCEND VIETNAM. THAT
ONE ENLISTED MAN REJECTED THE
MADNESS (THEREBY INVITING
SPECULATION ABOUT HIS SANITY AND
GALLANTRY) IS THE AFFIRMATION WHICH
PECULIARLY ELEVATES THIS HORROR
STORY. BUT IN THE END HE REMAINS A
HAUNTED, PERHAPS HUNTED FIGURE. IT
IS ON THE BATTLEFIELD WHERE AWARDS
FOR BRAVERY ARE WON. WILL THAT BE
THE ETERNALLY PRIMITIVE STORY OF
MODERN MAN?"
New York Post

CASUALTIES
OF
WAR

CASUALTIES OF WAR

Daniel Lang

POCKET BOOKS

New York   London   Toronto   Sydney   Tokyo

This material originally appeared in the October 18, 1969, issue of *The New Yorker*.

POCKET BOOKS, a division of Simon & Schuster Inc.
1230 Avenue of the Americas, New York, NY 10020

Published by arrangement with the Estate of the Author
Library of Congress Catalog Card Number: 75-105960

ISBN: 0-671-67253-3

First Pocket Books printing August 1989

10 9 8 7 6 5 4 3 2 1

POCKET and colophon are trademarks of
Simon & Schuster Inc.

Printed in the U.S.A.

To
William Shawn

CASUALTIES
OF
WAR

LIKE their predecessors in all wars, American veterans of the Vietnamese campaign who are coming home to civilian life have their heads filled with memories that may last the rest of their days, for, no matter how far from the front a man may have spent his time as a soldier, he will remember it as a special time, when, fleetingly, his daily existence appeared to approach the heroic. Former Private First Class Sven Eriksson—as I shall call him, since to use his actual name might add to the danger he may be in—has also come back with his memories, but he has no idea what the future will do to them. Honorably discharged in April, 1968, this new war veteran, who is twenty-four and comes from a small farming community in northwestern Minnesota, isn't even sure that he would care to hold on to his recollections, if it were possible for him to control his memory. Naturally, Eriksson's experiences in Vietnam were varied, and many of them impressed themselves vividly on his mind. Just seeing an Asian country, for instance, was an adventure, Eriksson says, its landscape so different from the frozen plains of his corner of Minnesota; he had never before splashed through paddy fields, he told me, or stood blinking in the sudden sunlessness of lush, entangled jungle, or wandered uncertainly through imprisoning fields of towering elephant grass. An infantryman, Eriksson saw a fair amount of action, so, if he chose, he could reminisce about strong points he helped take and fire fights in which he was pinned down, and one ambush, in particular, in which half his unit was wounded. But, as Eriksson unhesitatingly acknowledges, the fact is that when he thinks of his tour of duty in Vietnam it is always a single image that comes to his mind. The image is that of a Vietnamese peasant girl, two or three years younger than he was, whom he met, so to speak, on November 18, 1966, in a remote hamlet in the Central Highlands, a few miles west of the South China Sea. Eriksson and four other enlisted men were then on a reconnaissance patrol in the vi-

cinity of the girl's home. Eriksson considers himself
hazy about the girl's looks. He does remember,
though, that she had a prominent gold tooth, and
that her eyes, which were dark brown, could be particularly expressive. He also remembers that she was
wearing dusty earrings made of bluish glass; he noticed the trinkets because they gave off a dull glint
one bright afternoon when he was assigned to stand
guard over her. Like most rural women, she was
dressed in loose-fitting black pajamas. They ob-
scured her figure, Eriksson says, but he has the impression that she was slender and slight, and was
perhaps five feet two or three inches tall. For as long
as she lived, Eriksson did not know her name. He
learned it, eventually, when the girl's sister identi-
fied her at court-martial proceedings—proceedings
that Eriksson himself instigated and in which he
served as the government's chief witness. The girl's
name—her actual name—was Phan Thi Mao.
Eriksson never exchanged a word with her; neither
spoke the other's language. He knew Mao for
slightly more than twenty-four hours. They were her
last. The four soldiers with whom he was on patrol
raped and killed her, abandoning her body in mountain brush. One of the soldiers stabbed her three

times, and when defense counsel challenged Eriksson at the court-martial proceedings to describe the sound that the stabbings made, he testified, "Well, I've shot deer and I've gutted deer. It was just like when you stick a deer with a knife—sort of a thud—or something like this, sir."

ERIKSSON talked with me at his home in (I shall say) Minneapolis, where, since leaving the Army, he has been earning his living as a cabinetmaker at a local department store. He and his wife, Kirsten, have a neat, modest apartment of three rooms, its walls decorated with paintings by Mrs. Eriksson, a Sunday artist, who was present while we talked; she is twenty-three and is employed as a receptionist in an insurance office. The two have no children. They were married four years ago, shortly after Eriksson was drafted. They had known each other since childhood, their fathers having been neighboring farmers, who both had difficulty making ends meet. This was true of many farmers in the area, Mrs. Eriksson told me, adding that most of its inhabitants were of Scandinavian background. "It's a part of the country where we pride ourselves on not being demonstrative," she said. A small, pretty blonde with an alert, intelligent manner, she offered me coffee and cake the instant I set foot in the apartment. She was pleased, she told me, that I had asked to hear about the episode involving Mao. She herself had thus far been the only person with whom her husband had discussed it since returning from Vietnam, and even with her he had not gone into much detail. "It'll do him good to talk to someone else," she said, her tone lively and teasing. Sitting by himself on a sofa, Eriksson smiled somewhat ruefully, a deep dimple forming in one cheek. He is a short man of fair complexion, blond and blue-eyed, and he is not voluble. In the hours we spent together, there were intervals that may have lasted as long as a minute when he sat silent, a brooding expression on his face, before resuming his account. At the start, he spoke laconically, but gradually his natural reticence thawed out, and there were times—generally after one of his silences—when he produced such a burst of talk that it seemed to cost him an effort to bring it to a halt.

At the very outset, Eriksson told me that the last thing he wished to do was discuss Mao's murder in any legalistic vein. It was certainly possible to do so, as I knew for myself from having read the court record of the trials he had brought about: seven bulky volumes in the offices of the Clerk of Courts, U. S. Army Judiciary, in Falls Church, Virginia, which included Eriksson's testimony against the members of the patrol; their convictions and appeals; interminable correspondence between judges and opposing counsel; and depositions concerning the character of individual defendants. Having appeared as a witness before four tribunals in Vietnam, Eriksson told me, he had had his fill of the judicial process—of the dogged grillings by lawyers and the repeated strictures of judges insisting on precise answers to questions that were often vague. As far as he was concerned, Eriksson said, it had all seemed a morass of cleverness, but then, he conceded, he may well have entered the military courtroom in the Central Highlands, where the four trials were held, with unwarranted expectations, for it had been his hope that the trials would help him unravel his reactions to Mao's fate. Unreasonably, he granted, he had come into court with the idea that he and the others on hand would wonder aloud, in a kind of corporate searching, how it was possible for the young girl to meet the end she did. He had imagined that he would be able to ask how it was that he alone of the patrol had come to act as he had. He had wanted to tell of the way the episode with Mao had affected him, and why it was that he had felt impelled to report the others—four young Americans like him, each dependent on the others for survival deep in enemy territory. He had wanted to unburden himself of his doubts about whether he had done all he might have done for Mao in her travail—doubts that gnaw at him to this day. With me, he said, he trusted he would be able to go into these matters freely, but he had early discovered that in a court of law they were of little interest.

LAUNCHING into his unlegalistic account, Eriksson told me that it seemed clear to him in retrospect that he should have been prepared for Mao's death. It had been preceded by any number of similar occurrences. In one form or another, he said, they took place almost daily, but he was slow, or reluctant, to perceive that they were as much a part of the war as shells and targets were. Eriksson now believes he should have foreseen that sooner or later one of these incidents was bound to strike him with special, climactic force. He had scarcely landed in Vietnam, in October, 1966, when he was made aware of these occurrences, each of them apparently impulsive and unrelated to military strategy. He told me that beatings were common—random, routine kicks and cuffings that he saw G.I.s administer to the Vietnamese. Occasionally, official orders were used for justifying gratuitous acts of violence. Thus, early in his tour of duty, Eriksson recalled, G.I.s in his unit were empowered to shoot any Vietnamese violating a 7 P.M. curfew, but in practice it was largely a matter of individual discretion whether a soldier chose to fire at a stray Vietnamese hurrying home a few minutes late to his hootch—the American term for the mud-and-bamboo huts in which most natives lived. Similarly, it was permissible to shoot at any Vietnamese seen running, but, as Eriksson put it, "the line between walking and running could be very thin." The day after the one on which his squad was ambushed and half its members were wounded, several enemy prisoners were taken, and, in retaliation, two were summarily killed, "to serve as an example." A corporal who was still enraged over the ambush tried to strangle another of the prisoners; he had knotted a poncho, nooselike, around the cap-

18

tive's neck and was tightening it when a merciful lieutenant commanded him to desist.

Needless to say, Eriksson continued, the kind of behavior he was describing was by no means limited to Americans. The enemy did the same thing, and much of the evidence for this came from the Vietnamese themselves. They constantly reported rapes and kidnappings by the Vietcong; in fact, the Vietcong committed these crimes so indiscriminately that the victims were sometimes their own sympathizers. On one occasion that he knew of, Eriksson said, American troops, attracted by the familiar odor of decomposing bodies, had found a pit piled high with Vietnamese men and women who had been machine-gunned by the V.C. But, as Eriksson pointed out, he could not give me many such first-hand accounts of V.C. depredations. Necessarily, he said, he was in a position to speak only of the behavior of American soldiers, since they were the people he fought and lived with.

Ending the first of his brooding silences, Eriksson said, "From one day to the next, you could see for yourself changes coming over guys on our side—decent fellows, who wouldn't dream of calling an Oriental a 'gook' or a 'slopehead' back home. But they were halfway around the world now, in a strange country, where they couldn't tell who was their friend and who wasn't. Day after day, out on patrol, we'd come to a narrow dirt path leading through some shabby village, and the elders would welcome us and the children come running with smiles on their faces, waiting for the candy we'd give them. But at the other end of the path, just as we were leaving the village behind, the enemy would open up on us, and there was bitterness among us that the villagers hadn't given us warning. All that many of us could think at such times was that we were fools to be ready to die for people who defecated in public, whose food was dirtier than anything in our garbage cans back home. Thinking like that—well, as I say, it could change some fellows. It could keep them from believing that life was so valuable—anyone's life, I mean, even their own. I'm not saying that every fellow who roughed up a civilian liked himself for it—not that he'd admit in so many words that he didn't. But you could tell. Out of the blue, without being asked, he'd start defending what he'd done maybe hours ago by saying that, after all, it was no worse than what Charlie was doing. I heard that argument over and over again, and I could never buy it. It was like claiming that just because a drunken driver hit your friend, you had a right to get in your car and aim it at some pedestrian. Of course, I was a foot soldier all this time. I was operating in a forward area and probably seeing the war at its ugliest. In daylight it was search-and-destroy missions, and at night it was setting ambushes for the enemy. I discovered it's not difficult to kill a human being—in combat it's as instinctive as ducking bullets. You never knew whose turn it was to die, and that isn't how it was in rear areas. The farther back you got, the closer you approached the way people lived in civilian life."

ON November 16, 1966, the commanding officer of Eriksson's platoon, a Negro lieutenant, Harold Reilly (whose name, like every soldier's name in this account, has been changed), assigned him as one of five enlisted men who were to make up a reconnaissance patrol, its mission to comb a sector of the Central Highlands for signs of Vietcong activity. Testifying later in court, Lieutenant Reilly characterized the mission as "extremely dangerous," and said that to carry it out he had picked members of the best of the four squads in the platoon. Special care had been taken with the operation, he stated, since it had been conceived by the battalion command, a higher echelon than the company command, to which Reilly was ordinarily responsible. Explaining his choice of the patrol, Reilly testified, "These people, I felt, knew what they were doing, and a second reason was because the company commanding officer asked for good people." On the following afternoon, November 17th, the members of the newly formed patrol met in a corner of the platoon's headquarters area, near the village of My Tho, where, relaxed as they stood or sat on the ground, they listened to a briefing from their leader, who was seated on a low stool. He was Sergeant Tony Meserve, a slim, black-haired man of medium height who was twenty years old and came from a town in upstate New York, near the Canadian border. According to Eriksson, Meserve, who was assertive and confident, was both the patrol's youngest soldier and its most experienced one, being a volunteer of three years' standing who had fought in Vietnam for a year and had been decorated several times; he was due to go back to the United States in a month. The group's second-in-command was Ralph Clark, a corporal who came from a town near Philadelphia. He was twenty-two, a stringbean in physique, and blond, with eyes that were a pale, cold blue. Again according to Eriksson, Clark was given to quick movements and to seemingly abrupt decisions that reflected Meserve's thinking in an exaggerated form. The two other G.I.s in the combat team were a year younger than Eriksson, who was then twenty-two. They were cousins named Diaz—Rafael, known as Rafe, whose home was near Amarillo, Texas, and Manuel, who came from a town some distance north of Santa Fe, New Mexico. Eriksson remembers Rafe as a tall, swarthy, round-faced man with a disposition that was naturally sunny and amiable. As for Manuel, who was fair-skinned and stockier than his cousin, his manner was on the jumpy side. Like Clark, he was given to quick movements, but his behavior had nothing to do with embellishing Meserve's thinking. Manuel showed no initiative in that regard, Eriksson told me, his attitude toward authority being simple and automatic: he heeded it devoutly. In mild contrast, Rafe was capable of questioning authority, Eriksson said, but he generally wound up by going along with whoever seemed to be the leader—"just to keep from making trouble."

Returning to the patrol's briefing, Eriksson told

me that Meserve was all business as he plunged into his talk. Echoing the instructions that a battalion officer had given him earlier, the Sergeant informed the four men of the duties that each was expected to carry out, of the chain of command in the field, and of radio-communication arrangements with the platoon command, and then, consulting the grid coördinates of a map he was holding, the Sergeant described a precise westerly route that the patrol was to follow. It was to take them, ultimately, to Hill 192—a height, in the Bong Son valley, that overlooked a ravine laced with a cave complex, which was suspected of serving as a Vietcong hideout. But caves weren't all that the five men would be looking for. Bunkers, trenches, trails that were not marked on maps, caches of enemy equipment—these, too, were to be reconnaissance objectives. Naturally, Meserve said, if the men could spot any Vietcong in the open, that would be all to the good, but the patrol's orders—and these had been spelled out in no uncertain terms by the battalion command—were to avoid any shooting matches with the enemy except in self-defense; as a so-called pony patrol, he said, they were out to collect "early-warning" information concerning enemy intentions.

The men were to be gone five days, the Sergeant revealed—a fairly long time for a reconnaissance mission—and on hearing this Eriksson experienced a sense of exhilaration, just as he had at the prospect of far shorter patrols in which he had taken part. He felt that way, he explained, because out in the field, in territory that could turn hostile at any moment, the men in the patrol would be very much on their own, and this would be so even if a high-ranking officer were in charge. "You could never tell how a man was going to behave under pressure," Eriksson said. "He might turn out to be dumb or brave or to have a wonderful stock of jokes. Sure, there were always advance plans to do this or that, but they didn't often stand up in the field. The only thing you could count on out there was that the unexpected would happen." Usually, Eriksson said, it took time for the unexpected to develop, but now —more than half a day before the patrol was to leave platoon headquarters—it happened with stunning abruptness. It happened when the Sergeant, having delivered his instructions, concluded the briefing by telling the assembled men that they were going to have a good time on the mission, because he was going to see to it that they found themselves a girl and took her along "for the morale of the squad." For five days, the Sergeant said, they would avail themselves of her body, finally disposing of it, to keep the girl from ever accusing them of abduction and rape—both listed as capital crimes in the Uniform Code of Military Justice. Rafe later testified at his court-martial, "Meserve stated we would leave an hour ahead of time so that we would have time to find a woman to take with us on the mission. Meserve stated that we would get the woman for the purpose of boom boom, or sexual intercourse, and at the end of five days we would kill her." And in Manuel's testimony one finds: "After we were briefed by Meserve, he said that we would take a girl with us on patrol, or that we would try to take a girl with us to have some fun. . . . He said it would be good for the morale of the squad."

The Sergeant had made his announcement with a straight face, leaving his men to interpret it as they would. Clark at once greeted it with enthusiasm. The two Diazes laughed, either out of embarrassment, Eriksson conjectures, or because they thought Meserve was joking, in view of his remark about "the morale of the squad"—an old gag in the platoon. Eriksson told me that he himself reacted silently but that after Meserve and the men had broken up to go their separate ways until morning he sought out his friend Corporal Curly Rowan, a West Virginian, who had been in Vietnam, and with the platoon, just as long as Meserve had. Rowan listened with astonishment as Eriksson apprised him of the Sergeant's plan, but when Eriksson asked his friend whether he thought Meserve's statements should be reported to an officer before the patrol left camp, Rowan immediately shook his head, replying, as the court record shows, "Meserve wouldn't dare do such a fool thing." This incredulity notwithstanding, the news of Meserve's briefing left Rowan unhappy. The two men had arrived in Vietnam at the same time, and he had known Meserve as a considerate, agreeable man. However, in the last month or so, Rowan told Eriksson, the Sergeant, apparently undergoing changes, had exhibited a mean streak toward the Vietnamese; a couple of weeks before, Rowan said, Meserve had shot at and wounded one of them, giving as his reason afterward that he had "felt like it." "The way Curly talked about him, Meserve sounded as though he had become a kind of war casualty," Eriksson told me.

At four-thirty the following morning, Meserve diligently checked his men's gear at the edge of camp, seeing to it that their chow, star clusters, rounds of ammunition, smoke and hand grenades, and other supplies were in order. Once this was done, the patrol filed out of the camp in the faintly humid darkness, the men still uncertain of their leader's intent. Twenty minutes later, they knew what it was. By then, moving unhurriedly in the gray dusk, Meserve's squad had dutifully followed him two thousand metres to the east, which, as Eriksson and the others realized, was a flagrant deviation from the westward route the Sergeant had described so precisely at the briefing. By then, too, the men were approaching the hamlet of Cat Tuong, in the district of Phu My, and Eriksson was cursing himself for having listened to Rowan. In disbelief and confusion, his heart palpitating, Eriksson saw that Meserve was losing no time in carrying out his plan, for, with Clark at his heels, the Sergeant had embarked on a systematic search of the hamlet's hootches. The pair had emerged empty-handed from five or six of the huts when Rafe, ever his amiable, accommodating self, pointed to a white hootch ahead and called out, "There's a pretty girl in there! She has a gold tooth!"

Instantly, the Sergeant said, "That's the girl we'll find." Astounded by the enormity of his own suggestion, Rafe looked miserably at Manuel and Eriksson as Meserve and Clark, quickening their steps, made for the white hootch that contained the pretty girl with a gold tooth. While Eriksson, Manuel, and the now wretched Rafe hovered outside, Meserve and Clark entered the hut—Mao's home. They lingered in it longer than they had in the other hootches, but since Eriksson was standing outside the hut he is unable to describe what went on inside. However, Mao's sister, Phan Thi Loc, who was present, has done this at one of the trials. Translating the testimony of Loc, who was two years younger than Mao, an interpreter informed the court, "She said they come in, use flashlight and shone around the house and saw her mother's face and her sister's face and all of them wake up at the same time. It was six in morning and dark." The father was away in Phu My market, the interpreter went on. The mother wept and pleaded, and her daughters, clinging to one another, cowered against the wall. Loc was spared, but Mao was seized by the two soldiers, who bound her hands behind her back with a length of coconut rope. Reporting another of Loc's answers at the trial, the court interpreter stated, "She said her sister have gold tooth, right side in lower jaw."

When Meserve and Clark rejoined their comrades, Eriksson told me, they had the bound Mao well in tow. Clark was holding her elbow, and he pushed her forward when Meserve ordered the patrol to get moving. "Daylight was coming on fast, and he wanted the girl in the light as little as possible," Eriksson told me. "Helicopter crews might spot her." Before the patrol left the hamlet, a swarm of local children materialized, chattering agitatedly in a circle around Mao, and then out of the white hootch came Loc. The two sisters looked at each other. "Their eyes were terrified," Eriksson remembers. Departing from the hamlet with their prize, the soldiers moved west toward the main trail they should have been on. They had gone scarcely twenty metres when a cry of distress halted them. It came from Mao's mother, who was giving chase. Meserve testified at his court-martial, "The mother came out, like they always do, started crying, talking. We just tell them to *dee dee*"—meaning to go away. The mother, Eriksson told me, was waving a scarf and laboriously propelling herself forward. Panting, she finally reached the soldiers, indicating to them that the scarf was Mao's and that she would like her daughter to have it; the woman's cheeks were wet and her manner was imploring. It was an awkward moment, Eriksson said, and Clark terminated it. A smile spreading on his face, he took the scarf and stuffed it into Mao's mouth. In an affidavit that Manuel later signed, he stated, "Clark gagged the girl to keep her from yelling out. It was still dark in the area, and no civilians attempted to stop us." Leaving the mother behind, the patrol resumed its march, prodding Mao to match its stride. The hamlet was barely out of sight when Manuel, perhaps competing with Clark, untied Mao's hands, then slipped his pack from his shoulders and loaded it onto the girl's.

The five men and Mao kept up a steady pace. Meserve saw to that, for a brilliant sun had come up, its glare exposing the bizarre party as clearly as it did the landscape. "We were advancing through nice country," Eriksson told me. "We were on a plateau in the Highlands, and all around us were small mountain ranges, hazy and green. Below was a valley with a winding stream, and along its banks were paddy fields with neat little dikes around them. The country we were moving through was mostly all shades of green, but we also passed barren stretches and, here and there, places that had been browned by napalm. The land was very changeable. It would be open for a while, and then there'd be sections so thick with thorny vines tearing at our clothes that we couldn't see each other, even though we were spaced no farther apart than you and I are, right here in this room." Around eight o'clock, Meserve permitted his squad a half hour's break for chow. Mao was ungagged but was given no food; noticing that she was flushed and coughing slightly, Meserve handed her an aspirin. Only one piece of military action occurred that morning, and it could have been dispensed with. Gazing into the valley below, Rafe thought he spied a Vietnamese in a native type of straw hat standing in the stream. Deciding that he was looking at a V.C., Rafe let fly with a couple of rounds from his M-16 rifle. His target turned out to be the rump of a wallowing water buffalo, the animal raising itself from the shallow stream in clumsy panic and lumbering out of view. Rafe had flouted the order against unnecessary shooting, confirming Eriksson's observation that plans could mean little in the field and that out there any patrol was a unit only in theory. "We were each acting the way we had to," he told me. Meserve said nothing to Rafe; nor did he say anything to any of the others when, as the mission unfolded, they committed similar derelictions. Under cross-examination at his court-martial concerning this disregard of his commanding officer's instructions, the Sergeant stated, "Sir, most of the time everybody agrees with his C.O. Sometimes you have your disagreements, and sometimes you don't voice them, you keep them to yourself."

At ten-thirty, a short distance below the summit of Hill 192, Meserve found what he was looking for—a command post for the day. It was an abandoned hootch, eight feet square and eight feet high, with a window on the east side, a door on the west, and two slits facing north and south; there was a stream a few metres away, giving the patrol a ready source of water. The hootch contained a table, a low bench built against a wall, and tattered remnants of a straw mat strewn in a dark corner, and the dirt floor was littered with scrap metal, rocks, and cans. The structure was in a state of extreme disrepair, and had a number of large holes in its mud walls. However, it was essentially intact, and Meserve quickly converted it into a weapons depot, dumping ammunition stocks, and also food supplies, on its dirt floor. In addition, the hootch served as a place to hide Mao. Ordering Eriksson and Rafe to clean up the hootch, and leaving Mao in their charge, the Sergeant went off with Clark and Manuel to have a careful look around. In the hootch, Eriksson recalled, Mao, now relieved of Manuel's pack, watched him and Rafe heave out junk for a while, and then, unasked, the girl lent the G.I.s a hand. "She had no idea the kind of place she was helping to prepare," Eriksson said.

Meserve and the others returned an hour later, toward noon, and had a hearty snack, eating it outdoors, near the entrance to the hut. Sprawled on the ground after the meal, Meserve, refreshed, glanced at his fellows and then, with a knowing smile, indicated the partly ruined structure. "It's time for some fun," he said. Clark appeared to be beside himself with anticipation, Eriksson told me, and Manuel and Rafe appeared less so. He himself, he imagines, must have looked glum. "It was the way I felt," he said. "It was impossible for me to have any part of what I knew was about to take place." He suspects that Meserve sensed this, for before anything else happened the Sergeant confronted him, demanding to know whether he would enter the hootch when his turn came. Eriksson shook his head. Incensed, the Sergeant uttered the first of a series of threats. Unless Eriksson went along with the others, Meserve warned, he would run the risk of being reported "a friendly casualty." Clark seconded this vociferously, and both Diazes concentrated puzzled stares on the difficult member of the patrol. Eriksson shook his head again. "I had had enough of watching beatings and stranglings with ponchos," he told me. Rebuffed a second time, Meserve lashed out with an attack on Eriksson's manliness, deriding him as "queer" and "chicken." The attack didn't bother him, Eriksson told me, but it appears from the court record that it did affect Rafe, who testified that he could not have withstood the epithets he heard Meserve heap on Eriksson; it was his fear of such derision, Rafe stated, that caused him to join those who entered the hootch he had helped make tidy. Manuel gave similar testimony. "I was afraid of being ridiculed, sir," he told the prosecutor. Asked why, he answered, "O.K., let's say you are on a patrol. These guys right here are going to start laughing you out. Pretty soon, you're going to be an outcast from the platoon. 'That guy, he's scared of doing this, he's scared of doing that.' Everybody is going to make fun of you. When you go out on a patrol, you ain't going to be as good as you want to be, because these guys ain't helping you do anything. It is going to be yourself. There is going to be four people on that patrol and an individual."

Once Meserve had delivered his estimate of Eriksson's virility, the ill-fated bacchanal got under way. Just before it did, Eriksson moved away from the entrance to the hootch, where he had been standing, and sat down alone on the grassy turf to one side of the structure; periodically, he raised his field glasses to gaze at distant points. Cross-examined at Meserve's trial as to why he had shifted his position, Eriksson testified, "Well, sir, these gentlemen seemed to me—oh, I should say kind of enthused about what was going on. The whole thing made me sick to my stomach. I figured somebody would have to be out there for security, because there were V.C. in the area."

The Sergeant was the first man to enter the hootch, and soon, Eriksson told me, a high, piercing moan of pain and despair came from the girl. It repeated itself in waves, broken only, Eriksson assumed, by Mao's need to summon fresh breath.

After several minutes, the moan turned to a steady sobbing, and this did not cease until, after a half hour, Meserve reappeared in the open. He was shirtless; his face wore an expression of swaggering irresistibility. "She was real good—pretty clean," he said. Pointing to the hootch, he signalled to Rafe to be his successor, and Rafe, sparing himself ridicule, walked in. In court, Rafe said that he found Mao naked, lying on the table, her hands bound behind her back. "The girl looked so innocent, so calm," he testified. But Rafe stayed, and again the moan and the sobbing, slightly diminished, rose from the hootch. Outside, according to the court record, Clark was watching his comrade through a hole in the mud façade and letting out whoops of delight that mingled with Mao's cries. His manner became momentarily subdued when Meserve waved him in as the third man, but Clark was his jaunty self again when he returned. "I held a knife to her throat," he told the others. He displayed a hunting knife. It was ten inches long, and its handle was wrapped with tape that bore a pattern of tiny diamonds. The men were familiar with the knife; it had recently been given to Clark by a close friend in the platoon who had been wounded. As Manuel was going into the hootch, Mao's sounds could be heard, weak and conquered. The four soldiers' visitation lasted nearly an hour and a half, and two minutes after it was terminated the men, to conceal themselves from any Vietcong who might be in the vicinity, reëntered the hootch together. Eriksson was now with them, and he saw that Mao had retreated to a corner of the hut, frightened, watchful, her eyes glistening with tears, her presence made known chiefly by a cough that had grown more pronounced since morning. The girl was dressed and her hands had been freed. The men ate, again without feeding her, and reminisced about their communal feat, comparing Mao with other girls they had known, and talking about how long it had been since they had had a woman. After fifteen or twenty minutes, Meserve, as though he were finally bored with the topic, abruptly reminded the unit of its mission; he wanted the men to do some more reconnoitring that afternoon. This time, he said, it would be Clark who would stay behind to guard Mao and the weapons in the hootch.

The day continued eventful. Exploring the mountain further, often making their way through shoulder-high vegetation, Eriksson, Meserve, Manuel, and Rafe pushed on toward the summit. Though the men had to struggle for footing, Eriksson related, they made a point of keeping an eye on the stream that ran near the hootch; it had its source high up on the mountain, flowing down past a number of rice fields. After half an hour, their watch on the stream paid off, producing a more interesting sight than Rafe's water buffalo. Three Vietnamese were spotted walking along the edge of the water, and though they wore no uniforms, Meserve assumed they were V.C., and he and his men, including Eriksson, opened fire on them. None of the four hit anything, and the Sergeant radioed the platoon command for artillery support, which was quickly granted; the cooperation, Eriksson recalled, pleased Meserve no end, since it implicitly conferred an importance on the skirmish. Deciding to close in on the three Vietnamese, Meserve dispatched Eriksson and Rafe to the hootch to pick up a supply of smoke grenades. Arriving on the run, the two explained their errand to Clark, who heard the news eagerly, then pulled rank on Eriksson and ordered him to take his place in guarding the hootch. As Clark and Rafe left, Eriksson told me, he realized that he was about to exchange one kind of excitement for another—the encounter with the three Vietnamese, that is, for the quieter, more complicated ordeal of being alone with Mao. He was uncertain how he would act with her, he said, even though, oddly, he felt he knew her well; her cries, he said, had thrown him into a turmoil he had never before experienced. As he listened to her, he said, it had even crossed his mind to shoot her assailants, but then, he observed to me, "I'd have had the bodies of four men to justify." Asked in court for his thoughts during the period he had sat on the grassy turf, he testified, "Well, sir, I was wishing I wasn't in the situation I was in. I might say I was praying to God that if I ever got out of there alive I'd do everything I could to see that these men would pay for what they did."

Eriksson now lapsed into the longest of his silences with me, and when he spoke again, it was, for him, at great length. "When Mao saw me come into the hootch, she thought I was there to rape her," Eriksson said. "She began to weep, and backed away, cringing. She looked weary and ill, and she seemed to be getting more so by the minute. I had a feeling she had been injured in some way—not that I could tell. She had her black pajamas on. I gave her crackers and beef stew and water. It was her first food since she'd been taken away from her hamlet

—it had been still dark then, and here it was the middle of the afternoon. She ate, standing, and it was whimper, then eat, whimper, then eat. She kept looking at me, as though she was trying to guess what my game could be. When she finished eating, she mumbled something in Vietnamese; maybe it was 'Thank you'—I wouldn't know. And I told her, in English, 'I can't understand you.' I wanted to tell her other things. I wanted to say, 'I apologize to you for what's happened, but don't ever accept my apology or anyone else's for that. Please don't ask me to explain why they did it. I'll never know. You're hurt, I can see, but how are you? I mean, if I let you go, do you think you can make it home?' I wish Mao and I could have talked," Eriksson said, his voice tightening. "She might have helped me know what to do, instead of my having to figure it out alone—it was her life that was at stake. I stepped outside the hootch to be by myself awhile, and out there I could hear the muffled noise of artillery off in the distance. I had no idea where my unit was. I didn't know then that they were four hundred metres away, at the top of Hill 192, or that it would be a whole hour before they returned. It might have influenced my thinking if I'd had that information, but I'm not sure. As a disciplined soldier, I knew I wouldn't abandon the weapons in the hootch to the enemy, but, just the same, I was dizzy with thinking how to save Mao. I thought again of letting her go, but what would I tell Meserve when he got back? That this weak, coughing girl had overpowered me? Besides, she was in no condition to reach home or anywhere else. Then I thought of taking off together with her. We couldn't have gone very far, I realized, but it was going to be dark soon and we might find a hideout somewhere in the brush. After that, we'd have to stay out of sight until the third day of the patrol's mission—that was the day the patrol was supposed to rendezvous with another unit for fresh supplies. I knew the rendezvous spot, and if Mao and I could show up there at the right time, there was no question in my mind but that the fellows in the resupply squad would help us both. But I couldn't think any of my brainstorms through. I knew I had cut myself off from the rest of my patrol, refusing to go into that hootch, and I had this idea that the fellows were watching the place from the brush, waiting for me to make just one false move with Mao. I had this picture that when we did, they'd fire at us, or, at least, Meserve would have me up on charges of desertion. The guys would back him up, of course. They'd say there had never been a girl with the patrol, and I'd be left looking crazy."

Shifting uneasily on the sofa, Eriksson went on, "When I stepped back into the hootch, I saw that Mao had made up her mind that I wasn't going to harm her. She had stopped whimpering, and there was even a little look of trust in her eyes. There shouldn't have been, because I had decided, outside, that there wasn't a thing in the world I could do for her. It was the hardest decision I've ever had to make, and it couldn't have been the best possible one, or Mao wouldn't be gone today."

In the time that elapsed before the patrol's return, Eriksson said, Mao's condition worsened noticeably. The men found her feverish and coughing, and Clark was all for rescheduling her death hour to that evening. Meserve, however, counselled patience. A good night's rest might do wonders for Mao's health, he pointed out, in which case he, for one, wouldn't mind revisiting her in the morning. Rafe subsequently testified that the Sergeant was in an expansive mood, cheerfully observing to his men that it wasn't every day he could rate artillery support and have himself a woman as well. The patrol and Mao shared the hootch that night, the girl spending it in a corner by herself. The soldiers set up a night watch, each man pulling guard duty outside in the moonlight, alert for any lurking enemy. Mao coughed throughout the night, and at one point, Eriksson recalls, Clark again urged that the girl be finished off forthwith. Eriksson said, "He told Meserve her coughing was going to give away our position, but I didn't think it was Charlie he had on his mind. I thought he wanted to destroy living evidence."

IN the morning, everyone got up shortly after six, and it wasn't long before Mao's fate was sealed. "Events happened fast that day," Eriksson said. The first of them, he told me, was that Mao woke up less alluring than when she had gone to bed. Her fever and coughing had increased overnight, he said, and that didn't do her cause any good. Meserve, he noticed, paid scarcely any attention to her. The Sergeant seemed more attracted by the possibility of military action, to judge by the speed with which he had his charges break camp. His last order before they left was to send Eriksson, Rafe, and Manuel to fetch the day's supply of water from the stream.

When they returned, Eriksson told me, they discovered that Clark was no longer alone in advocating Mao's early demise. Meserve was now an ally, he and his second-in-command apparently having arrived at a meeting of minds while the others were filling the patrol's canteens. As Mao stood listening, mute and uncomprehending, Meserve said that she had to be got out of the way; if they ran into action, he pointed out, she would be a hindrance, and even if they didn't, helicopter crews scouting the area might want to know who she was. All that awaited decision, Meserve went on, was the moment and method of the girl's murder, but, whatever was settled on, the Sergeant's thought was to have Eriksson do the job; if Eriksson refused, Meserve said, he would be reported as K.I.A.—killed in action. Manuel later told agents of the Army's Criminal Investigation Division, "Meserve said to Eriksson that inasmuch as he did not do anything to the girl [the day before], Eriksson would have to kill the girl, but Eriksson said that he would not have anything to do with that." Meserve, however, didn't follow through on his threat. To Eriksson's astonishment and deep relief, the Sergeant abruptly shifted his attention to the Diazes, asking first Rafe and then

Manuel to carry out the murder. "Both refused," Eriksson said. "They were very definite. It excited me." Impatiently, Clark volunteered his services, but Meserve wouldn't have that, insisting that they collaborate. Clark could knife the girl from the front, the Sergeant said, while he bayoneted her from behind; the body would then be tossed over a cliff from the summit of Hill 192, where the patrol had reconnoitred the previous day. Accordingly, at nine the group struck out for the cliff. The climb took longer than it had the day before, the men's pace slowed by the packs they bore. This morning, Manuel carried his own. Serving as radioman, he was in the vanguard with Meserve and Clark; Mao walked ten metres behind, wearily ascending the rugged terrain, with Rafe as her forward guard and Eriksson bringing up the rear. It took an hour to negotiate the climb, and the group had barely attained the ridge when Rafe, his eyes sweeping the vista below, saw five Vietnamese in peasant dress making their way along a mountain trail toward the paddy fields near the stream. The Vietnamese proved to be V.C., for the moment they were aware that they had been seen they fired at the patrol with small arms, then changed their direction and passed temporarily out of sight. Meserve at once radioed the platoon command, reaching Lieutenant Reilly, to whom he suggested that the V.C. be ambushed. Agreeing, the Lieutenant said that he would order another squad, operating at the base of the mountain, to coördinate its movements with those of Meserve's patrol, and that he would also dispatch two other squads to the area. In addition, Meserve learned that he was again to be the recipient of artillery support; in a short while, Reilly said, helicopter gunships—aircraft equipped with rocket artillery and machine guns —would be in the area. "It was going to be a big outlay, considering the few men we were up against," Eriksson said. Ordinarily, he conjectured, the promise of such generous support would have cheered Meserve, but Mao's presence seemed to confuse matters. Glancing at the girl with distaste, the Sergeant ordered Eriksson and Rafe to stay with her on the ridge, whereupon he, Clark, and Manuel began a cautious descent of the mountain, their purpose to stalk the Vietcong. Thirty metres down, they came to a curiously shaped rock formation composed of two jutting ledges. Using the upper one as a vantage point, they spied the small band of V.C. making slow progress toward the refuge of the cave complex, which was three hundred metres away, almost at the bottom of the ravine. But the Sergeant did nothing about the escaping V.C., for he was now powerfully distracted from the enemy; in the distance, still inaudible and looking miniaturized, were four approaching gunships. Acting fast, he sent Manuel backtracking to the summit to tell Eriksson and Rafe to report to him with Mao. In ten minutes, they were all together again; by then, too, the helicopters had grown larger and their engines were faintly audible. Rafe later testified, "There were helicopters flying around, and everyone was getting jumpy about having the girl."

Before Meserve could devise any next step, Clark took hold of Mao's arm. "Let's kill her and get it over with," he said, according to the court record.

"All right, go ahead," Meserve said, and he instantly turned his attention to the enemy, ordering Eriksson to the lower ledge of rock while he and Manuel returned to the upper one, with Rafe to their rear.

Rafe was the man closest to Clark and Mao—only a few metres away—and because he was, his testimony concerning the events that now took place carried special weight with the court. He stated at the trial, "From where I was, I observed Clark grab the girl by the arm and take her into the bushes nearby . . . I saw that Clark had his hunting knife hidden in one of his hands." It was in the next seconds that deer-gutting sounds issued from the bushes. "I then heard the girl cry out, but not too loud," Rafe continued. "Clark came back to where we were. Meserve asked him if he had finished the girl." Clark had just replied yes when Mao, like a wounded apparition, was seen crawling rapidly downhill and then disappearing into the thick foliage. As Rafe recounted it, "Meserve saw her and said, 'There she goes.' Clark said, 'Why, that bitch, I stabbed her more than twice.' Meserve told us all to shoot her before she could get away. We were all told to look for the girl." All five men shot, but Eriksson aimed his weapon—a grenade launcher, which looks like a shotgun—down into the valley, away from the general direction of Mao. In addition, Rafe flatly said, "Eriksson could not see the girl," despite which, Rafe also testified, "Eriksson stated, 'Oh, no,' like he regretted that he had fired." Rafe himself let go with a burst from his M-16, which, inexplicably, caused his rifle to jam. However, he did call Clark's attention to a bush directly ahead. It was rustling. "I couldn't tell whether it was Charlie or the girl," Rafe testified. Clark, who was several metres in front of Rafe, yelled back to him that it was the girl. "I saw him raise his rifle," Rafe stated, adding that he then started toward Clark. Moving in on the bush, Clark blazed away with his M-16, and at once the rustling foliage grew still. "You want her gold tooth?" Clark called over his shoulder to Rafe, who was then, he testified, a foot away and was staring, aghast, at Mao. "When I got up to the girl, I saw that her head was partially blown away," he testified. "She was dead, I'm sure."

Immediately after the murder, Eriksson told me, the men appeared to assume a self-protective air of disbelief at what had taken place. Straggling uphill, he said, they gravitated toward their leader, who stood, unflustered, near the jutting rock formation, surveying the combat situation. It had built up sharply. The gunships were now unmistakably in the area, their motors sending up a storm of noise as the machines hovered low and their crews searched out the enemy. Now the V.C., flushed from their temporary hideout, continued to beat a desperate retreat, relying on sniper fire to fend off their attackers, who were converging on them from both sides of the stream. Small artillery spotter planes had arrived, heralding the imminent use of ground-artillery support. The court record attests that it was in the midst of this encircling racket that Meserve chose to initiate radio contact with Lieutenant Reilly, the burden of the Sergeant's message being that he wanted to report "one V.C., K.I.A." Under cross-examination at Meserve's court-martial, Reilly, appearing as a defense witness, testified, "Sergeant Meserve called me up and informed me in the middle of the fire fight that a girl was fleeing up the side of the mountain, and I informed him to get the girl. He called me back in a few minutes, or a couple of minutes, and informed me that he could not catch the girl, that he had had to shoot her. . . . I called him back and commended him on the job that he did and reported it, in turn, to the company headquarters."

Meserve fought well that day. With Mao out of the way, he was able to concentrate on the action at hand, managing his patrol, working in concert with the other squads, and helping to guide the diving gunships, whose presence he now welcomed. Among them, Eriksson said, these sizable elements, advancing toward the cave complex, succeeded in killing one V.C. and wounding another. Two escaped, and the fifth man made it to the caves, where he holed up for a last-ditch stand. The man was never captured, Eriksson said, despite the fact that he became the single target of the gunships' rockets and the infantry's bullets and grenades. Moreover, Eriksson told me, the enemy soldier inflicted casualties on the infantrymen deployed around the cave complex, which was some two hundred metres long and had numerous mouths. At the time the fifth V.C. entered the caves, he said, the patrol had long ago left the vicinity of the curiously shaped rock formation, and had descended so deep into the valley that the men were practically able to touch the thick, rough outer walls of the caves. Meserve, Clark, and Manuel, together with members of the other squads, were shooting away at the solitary V.C., who was behind an aperture that measured perhaps six inches wide and a couple of inches high. As for himself, Eriksson told me, Meserve had ordered him to a ledge from which he could overlook the complex as he trained his grenade launcher on two cave mouths in particular, either one of which, the Sergeant thought, could afford the entombed V.C. an exit. For Rafe, the fighting had ended an hour earlier— well before the patrol reached the cave complex.

As the men had raced to get there, clambering and sliding, Rafe had slipped and fallen from a ledge, dislocating an elbow and a shoulder. Evacuated by a medical helicopter, he was flown to a hospital at Qui Nhon. There, corpsmen deposited him on a bed alongside that of a battalion officer he knew and liked. At Rafe's court-martial, it was disclosed that for several days the two patients in the hospital ward seemingly talked about whatever came into their heads but that Rafe never mentioned Mao. Testifying in his own defense, Rafe stated, "I was afraid to tell [the officer], because I might be the only one who brought it up. I didn't know Eriksson brought it up. I wanted to find out first what Meserve and Clark might do."

The fire fight in the ravine lasted several hours, the attackers finally breaking off after dark. The holed-up V.C. (who escaped the following morning) wounded five Americans, and Meserve displayed considerable courage in rescuing the most seriously injured of them, a G.I. whose ammunition pouch, girding his midriff, had exploded as the result of a hit. "The poor guy's guts were out," Eriksson said. "It was as though he had shot himself with two rounds of his own ammo." The wounded man lay helpless, directly in front of the small opening from which the V.C. was shooting, and Meserve, braving a fusillade of bullets, crept forward and pulled the man out of the V.C.'s line of fire. For this action, Meserve was nominated for a Bronze Star.

Eriksson had no occasion to fire his grenade launcher, and that was just as well, he told me, since his mind was on Mao—on the part of the war that, as he put it, "had got to me." Perched on the mountainside, listening to the gunfire and the helicopters, he found his thoughts returning repeatedly to the fact that Rafe and Manuel had refused to kill the girl. Transitory though their show of character may have been, he said, it encouraged him in reaching a private resolve, for as he kept watch above the cave complex, Eriksson told me, he was suddenly seized with the overwhelming realization that unless he took it upon himself to speak out, the fact of Mao's death would remain a secret. "No one would ever know what had become of her!" he exclaimed. "Who else would tell but myself? All the others in the patrol had raped or killed her. I knew I wouldn't rest until something was done about Mao's murder. It was the least I could do—I had failed her in so many ways. The only thing that could stop me was if I became a friendly casualty."

LOOKING back, Eriksson thinks that the small band of V.C. may have rescued him from Meserve. The outmanned, outgunned enemy put up so strong a fight, he said, that the Sergeant, Clark, and Manuel ran out of ammunition, and the patrol had to interrupt its five-day mission long enough to go back for fresh supplies of bullets and grenades. This meant going to platoon headquarters—the home of four squads, and only a few minutes' walk from company headquarters, where there were officers who outranked Reilly, the platoon's lone lieutenant. Arriving at the platoon area, Eriksson told me, he felt as though he had reached the promised land; the anxiety in which he had lived the past two days yielded to what he described as an almost tangible sense of safety. Since the patrol would be going out again, Eriksson said, he knew he had to act fast, but that seemed no big deal. In the first place, he wanted to act fast, and, besides, he had no doubt that once he did act, there would be fast results. Once he was inside the camp perimeter, he assumed, it would be a simple matter to bring Meserve and the others to judgment. All he need do, he believed, was report that they had committed rape and murder, and the military authorities would investigate with the same alacrity that civilian authorities are expected to show in such situations. During his first hour back in camp, he recalls, no one could have persuaded him otherwise.

In any event, Eriksson went on, he lost little time in seeking out his friend Curly Rowan to tell him the story of Mao. He had barely begun it, however, when Clark, seeing the two in conversation, descended on them, demanding to know what they were talking about. "We made up something to get him to go away," Eriksson told me. "He had a wild manner—he couldn't stand still, and his eyes looked every which way. All of us in the patrol had long ago stopped pretending nothing horrible had happened. All of us had come back scared and upset, but Clark, I thought, showed it the most." Once Clark had left them, Eriksson continued with his story, feeling an immense relief when he had finished telling it. "At last, someone outside the patrol knew of Mao," he said. He had no illusion, though, that Rowan himself could do much about what he had just learned, but at that, Eriksson said, his friend did what he could, immediately relaying news of the murder to the sergeant of his own squad. In turn, the sergeant passed the news on to Lieutenant Reilly, who sent for Eriksson.

Arriving at the austere hootch that Reilly used as a command post, Eriksson told me, he imagined that the Lieutenant, if only conversationally, would express dismay over the murder. No such dismay was expressed. Instead, to Eriksson's astonishment, Reilly chose that moment to offer a reminiscence. Calmly and easily, he told Eriksson about an experience that he had undergone three years earlier, when he drove his wife, also a Negro, to an Alabama hospital to have their first child. She was in an advanced state of labor, the Lieutenant related, but she had been refused admittance to the hospital, on racial grounds, and she had eventually had her baby on the floor of its reception room. Wild with rage, Reilly had tried to wreck the place, whereupon hospital orderlies summoned the police, and the new father was arrested and jailed. In his cell, Reilly went on, he had made plans to shoot various officials at the hospital, but when he was finally released he gave up the idea of vengeance. "By the time I got out of jail," he told Eriksson, "I was saying to myself, 'What's happened is the way things are, so why try to buck the system?' And take it from me, Eriksson, it's even more hopeless to try to buck it in the middle of a war—there's more of a system then than ever. Better relax about that Vietnamese girl, Eriksson. The kind of thing that happened to her—what else can you expect in a combat zone?" His recollection out of the way, the Lieutenant informed Eriksson that the patrol, having replenished its ammunition stocks, would be leaving camp at any moment to resume its five-day mission. Eriksson wouldn't be going along, though; the Lieutenant had assigned another G.I. in his stead. Acknowledging the danger in which Eriksson had placed himself, the Lieutenant told him, "If I sent you out with that patrol, you'd never make it back."

As the court transcript shows, Reilly didn't let matters rest there. The atrocity that Eriksson had reported was too big for that. Reilly was aware that if it came to public knowledge it would tarnish the image of the officers commanding the platoon, the company, the battalion, perhaps even the regiment; the officers might be made to appear incapable of controlling the conduct of the men in their commands. Reilly's immediate superior, Captain Otto Vorst, as was later brought out in court, was out in the field at the time on "a tactical problem." He was not due back until November 22nd, the day Meserve's patrol was scheduled to conclude its mission.

The Captain—a "lifer," or career Army man—
had left instructions that he was to be sent urgent
messages only, but shortly after Eriksson took leave
of Reilly, the Lieutenant, confident that the murder
merited his superior's attention, radioed word of it
to Vorst. As it happened, the Captain heard about it
from a second source as well—from Eriksson
himself. Out on a search-and-destroy mission the
morning after leaving Meserve's command, Eriksson
told me, he encountered a small group of American
military men reconnoitring the vicinity of the cave
complex. Vorst was in the group, and Eriksson, de-
taching himself from his unit, went up to the Captain and told him about Mao. "Leave it to me. I'll
handle everything," Vorst said. A moment later, the
two groups went off in different directions.

On November 22nd, Meserve, Clark, and Manuel, weary from their five-day stint (Rafe was still
hospitalized), had scarcely dropped into their foxholes back in the platoon area when they were ordered to appear at Captain Vorst's command post
—a hootch somewhat larger than Reilly's but
equally bare. They found the company commander,
who had himself only just returned, waiting impatiently to confront them with Eriksson's report. In

his affidavit for Army investigators, Manuel gave what is probably a comprehensive account of the confrontation that took place in the Captain's quarters. "This was about 1400 hours," Manuel stated. "Captain Vorst handed Meserve a piece of paper with three words printed on it—Kidnapping, Rape, Murder. We all looked at the paper, and he asked us what this was all about. At first, we all denied any knowledge about it. He first asked Sergeant Meserve, 'Do you know anything about this?' To which Meserve said, 'We don't know what you're talking about.' He then directed the same question to all of us, 'Do you people know what you've done up there?' Captain Vorst then asked me did I know what would or could happen to me. I said, 'Probably the firing squad, sir.' He then said something to the effect, 'I could send you all back to the States for courts-martial,' or he could court-martial us out here and still have a firing squad. Then the C.O. said something to the effect, 'You people acted like animals up there and do not deserve to live.' He said he would have never learned about this but one man had the balls to tell [the officers] about it. Then he proceeded to tell us that if anything happened to Eriksson, our souls would belong to him." Possibly to help them retain their souls, Vorst announced that he was breaking up the patrol. Rafe, hospitalized at Qui Nhon, was already accounted for; Clark was to take a relatively rear-area post, at battalion headquarters; Meserve was to be shifted to another platoon. Only Manuel would remain anywhere near Eriksson; he was being reassigned to a different squad in the same platoon.

Eriksson saw Vorst shortly after the three soldiers left the company command post. At the time, Eriksson told me, he had no idea that the Captain had chewed them out. If he had known this, he thinks, he might have realized then, as he did later, that the Captain was in a bind; that is, he was torn between the dictates of his conscience, which condemned the crime, and concern for his Army career, which, Eriksson later discovered, the battalion commander —who outranked Vorst, and who was also a "lifer"—was in the habit of admonishing the Captain to bear in mind. Initially, however, Eriksson discerned no signs of inner conflict in Vorst. As far as he could make out, the company C.O. held a clear, uncomplicated view of the crime, and that view was that its repercussions should be kept to a minimum. "That word 'handle'!" Eriksson said reminiscently. "Three times I saw the C.O. about Mao, and three times he used it—'I'll handle everything,' 'I'll handle everything,' 'I'll handle everything.' Maybe he did, but not in a way that had anything to do with anyone's making amends." At his meeting with Vorst the day of the Captain's return, he went on, he noticed that—like Reilly, who was present—the company commander failed to deplore the murder, and instead stressed its potentialities as a scandal. Reilly later testified in court, "Captain Vorst stated to Eriksson, 'I guess you realize how serious this incident is, and that it could cause an international issue.' Eriksson stated that's why he reported the incident—because he knew it was serious. Eriksson also stated that the entire taking of the girl, the rape, and killing of the girl were preplanned . . . that he [had] thought [at first] the men were just joking about really completing the acts." Throughout, Eriksson told me, he had the distinct impression that his position and Vorst's were at variance. Despite Vorst's generally negative tone, Eriksson said, he believed that the company commander would eventually take steps to bring Meserve and the others to justice. At one point, Eriksson recalled, the Captain warned him that if the incident did result in courts-martial, he might face rough going on the witness stand. When Eriksson replied that he was prepared to take his chances on that, Vorst asked whether Eriksson might not care to transfer out of the company—or, for that matter, out of the infantry altogether. Eriksson replied that he wouldn't mind a change—not that it would deter him from pressing charges. He wouldn't mind being a door gunner aboard a helicopter, he told Vorst, citing as his qualifications for such a post that he had been trained as a machine gunner and that he was fond of flying. Vorst filled out transfer forms, and Eriksson signed them. As he was leaving, he told me, the Captain called out reassuringly, "I'll handle everything!"

When Eriksson heard nothing from Vorst for four days, he sought an interview, which was granted. It was the final talk between the two men. They were alone this time, Eriksson told me, and when Eriksson inquired what progress there had been in the murder case, the Captain seemed not to hear but posed a series of questions. He was merely asking, Vorst said, but had Eriksson really thought through what he was doing in pushing his charges? Had he taken into account the amount of suffering that

Americans had already undergone in behalf of the Vietnamese? Had he stopped to think of the consequences to himself of accusing four fellow-G.I.s— thereby adding to that suffering? Besides, what if the four were court-martialled and found guilty? Did Eriksson know that military judges and jurors were notoriously lenient in their sentencing? Unlike their civilian counterparts, Vorst said, the law officers (the term by which military judges were known) and members of the court (as jurors were known) had a sympathetic understanding of the pressures a combat man faced in risking his life daily; military jurists didn't expect foot soldiers to be on their best behavior in a war zone. Here, the C.O. went on, it was mild sentences that were the order of the day, and, what was more, they became even milder when they were up for review; safe and professionally idealistic back home, he said, the legal experts of military appellate bodies invariably looked with suspicion upon the administration of justice in war zones. Thus, Vorst concluded, coming to the last of his questions, if the men in the patrol were actually convicted, Eriksson could anticipate their being freed in short order, and when that happened Eriksson himself might not feel so free—for was it really inconceivable that one or more of the ex-convicts would seek revenge? And wasn't it just possible that the victim might not necessarily be Eriksson himself but, rather, his new bride? Eriksson stated in court, "Captain Vorst said that the men would get off with hardly any or no sentence at all, then myself and my family would really have something to worry about."

IN the weeks immediately following Mao's death, Eriksson's home continued to be the platoon area, and his routine consisted of patrols—search-and-destroy by day, ambush by night. These were always demanding and hazardous, yet they could not distract him from the intense feeling of frustration that now beset him. After his last talk with Vorst, he told me that frustration was always with him—eating at him, keeping him remote from his fellow-G.I.s, costing him sleep. Lying awake nights, listening to Asian birdsong and the squealing of monkeys in the jungle nearby, he said, he found himself constantly mulling over the phenomenon of military discipline —the chain-of-command system. As in all armies, he believed, it pervaded every facet of military life, embracing officers and enlisted men, volunteers and draftees, and, for that matter, men with college degrees, like Vorst and Reilly, and men with meagre educations, like Meserve and him. He was at his wit's end for a way to circumvent the system, Eriksson told me, because he was convinced that it was this system that lay at the heart of his difficulties. He saw now how wrong he had been in thinking that a report of rape and murder would evoke instant action, as in civilian life. In the Army, he had discovered, that kind of action depended entirely on the discretion of one's superior—unless it was possible to figure out some way of bypassing him. It was maddening, Eriksson said, to realize that military discipline threatened to make Mao its victim again, just as it had on Hill 192, when all that certified Meserve's orders was his rank as sergeant. "They scare that discipline into you in basic training," Eriksson told me. "It's obey the man over you, follow the chain of command, or into the stockade you go." Something that added to his feeling of frustration in those trying weeks was that he could not find it within himself to single out Vorst as the arch-villain, from whom all evil flowed. Eriksson said to me, "It only looked as though he was the one out to do everything in, but the C.O., I knew, had someone over him, and *his* superior had a superior. That was the thing about the chain of command—you couldn't tell who was to blame for what. It had nothing to do with a man's being responsible for his own behavior. Just as long as he stayed in line, just as long as he kept the set-up going, he could do whatever he wanted."

Perhaps the most jarring of all the discoveries he made during this unhappy period, Eriksson told me, was that his fellow-G.I.s took a dim view of his efforts in behalf of Mao. To be sure, there were a few individuals, like Rowan, who shared his outlook, but the great majority saw things the way their officers did. Time and again, at chow or during a break out in the field, someone would tell him (as Vorst had told him) that it was pointless to throw good lives after bad by having Meserve and the others up on charges, since (as Reilly had said) violence was the language of war, and, naturally, it could not always be controlled. Continually, Eriksson recalls, he heard the familiar argument that the V.C. also kidnapped, raped, murdered. "Hey, Sven, how do you know that girl wasn't a V.C.?" an Oklahoma rifleman asked one night as he and Eriksson were settling down to sleep in their foxholes. Each day, Eriksson said, he felt as though he were at war with war, a troublemaker out to undermine some careful, desperate code of survival. When he first got back from Hill 192, he said, he had imagined that it might have been his peculiar misfortune to draw a patrol made up of psychopaths, but now each time a new G.I. rallied to the patrol's defense that idea seemed less tenable. "Listening to the fellows, I had the feeling there might be any number of Meserves and Clarks around me," he said. "It was like living in an overorganized jungle—full of names, ranks, and serial numbers but not much else."

Dispiriting though he found the atmosphere in the platoon area, Eriksson went on, there were traces of conscience there. It took him a while to realize this, he said, and, curiously, he became persuaded of its prevalence as a result of thinking about Vorst's negative "handling." As he went over it in his mind for the hundredth time, he began to suspect the existence of cracks in the Captain's seemingly certain, untroubled façade. If there weren't any, Eriksson asked himself, why hadn't the C.O. simply told him to bug off from the word go? Why had he bothered to discuss Mao with him three times? Nor could the concern that the C.O. had shown for Eriksson's safety be explained unless those cracks existed. Why else had Vorst seen fit to reshuffle the patrol, leaving only Manuel within shooting distance, so to speak? And then there was Vorst's invitation to Eriksson to transfer out of the company. It seemed like a deal, but why was it, Eriksson asked himself, that a captain should feel constrained to bargain with a lowly enlisted man? Why make all this effort to dismiss the death of an unknown peasant girl if it weren't that the C.O. recognized that there were forces of conscience that might have to be contended with? Thinking along these lines, Eriksson said, he arrived at a kind of strategy in regard to Mao. "Whatever I could do about her depended on finding someone with both the rank and the conscience to help me," he told me. "Otherwise, I'd stay boxed in by the chain of command."

On the last day of November, Eriksson was in a patrol that was chasing two or three V.C. down a trail between two hedgerows when the patrol was suddenly fired upon from one side. "Hit it!" the patrol leader shouted, and his men hit the ground, the bullets from the still invisible attackers raising columns of dust all around the flattened G.I.s. In a matter of seconds, the shooting broke off, and another patrol, consisting of another squad in Reilly's platoon, emerged from behind the hedgerow. Eriksson's patrol leader delivered a tongue-lashing to his counterpart, who apologized. It had all been a mistake, he said—he and his men had been dozing when the sound of running feet aroused them, and instinctively they had assumed it was the enemy. He had stopped the shooting as soon as he heard an American voice yell "Hit it!" Still fuming as the two patrols stood facing each other awkwardly, Eriksson's sergeant declared that in all the time he had spent in Vietnam he had never before experienced any such "mistake." As Eriksson waited for his sergeant to cool off, he idly scanned the men in the other squad, his eyes stopping abruptly when they met the expressionless gaze of a familiar face. "It was Manuel," Eriksson told me. "We just looked at each other, without saying hello. Seeing him made me think at once of two questions I would have liked to ask him or his sergeant. Just who, I wanted to ask, was the man in Manuel's patrol who started the shooting? And who was the man who fired the last shot? I couldn't even guess at the answers—not without knowing what kind of jam Manuel thought he was in."

Whatever the answers, Captain Vorst saw to it that Eriksson left his command early the following morning, sending the enlisted man seventy miles away to Camp Radcliff, the 1st Cavalry (Airmobile) Division base, near the small city of An Khe. Eriksson was to remain there until his reassignment as a door gunner came through, Vorst having sent his transfer papers on for official approval by the helicopter command. In the meantime, Eriksson's orders placed him on temporary duty with a carpentry detail that was constructing additional housing for the base, whose population came to twenty thousand. Eriksson was delighted with this duty, since he had had a passion for carpentry all his life. However, he welcomed the shift to Radcliff for a more important reason. He was confident, he told me, that he stood a better chance of finding help there than in the confines of the platoon area. Far from where the daily, relentless fighting was going on, he pointed out, Radcliff was probably less disposed to take gratuitous violence in stride; besides, there were infinitely more people at the division base, and that gave him a better chance of finding the effective ally he needed. "From the minute I got to Radcliff, I was on the lookout for him, whoever he might turn out to be," Eriksson said.

His break came after just a week—by accident, which was the only way it could come. Late one afternoon, when he and about twenty other G.I.s putting up a barracks were about to knock off for the day, he saw a fellow-carpenter, Boyd Greenacre, detach himself from the crew to have a talk with a passing chaplain, a blond, long-nosed six-footer wearing a captain's bars; the two men, Eriksson could see, were on cordial terms. Eriksson had never laid eyes on the chaplain before. For that matter, he said, he knew almost nothing about Greenacre—only that he was a cowboy from Arizona, a wiry type, who put in a good day's work as a carpenter and didn't have much to say. Now, watching the chaplain depart, Eriksson decided that Greenacre was very much worth cultivating. Eriksson was determined to meet the Arizonan's friend, he told me, for he had a feeling that the long-nosed chaplain was the man who would help him bring Mao's case to light. Seeing him and Greenacre chatting together, Eriksson went on, had made him realize that the only chance he had of escaping the chain of command was through a chaplain. Actually, Eriksson told me, he had once asked Reilly for permission to discuss Mao's murder with a chaplain, but the Lieutenant had discouraged the idea. Perhaps, Eriksson said, he remembered that idea just then because of his recent stewing about Vorst and conscience. At any rate, he felt that he was on the right track, since chaplains were professionally concerned with conscience. "Conscience was one thing that crossed over from civilian life to war," he said. "It was as much a part of us as our legs and arms."

His spirits on the upswing, Eriksson set about trying to meet the chaplain. "It had to be him, and no other chaplain," he recalled, smiling. "And it had to be Boyd Greenacre who would introduce me. That was how my hunch went, and I didn't dare change it in any way." Eriksson moved cautiously. He didn't see how he could just walk up to Greenacre and state his business. Greenacre might react disapprovingly, as the fellows in the platoon had— or, for all Eriksson knew, Greenacre might turn out to be Meserve's best friend. As a result, Eriksson spent the next two days surreptitiously doing a kind of security check on Greenacre's character. "I needed more of an impression of Boyd than I had," Eriksson said. "What if he refused to arrange an introduction for me? I had to know whether he could at least be trusted to keep quiet about what I was up to." As indirectly and offhandedly as he could, Eriksson sounded out various members of the work detail about Greenacre—none of whom, he remarked, he knew any better than he knew the Arizonan. He remembers that he talked with one of them while they were both shaving, and that in shooting the breeze with another he led the conversation around to Greenacre when the man mentioned that Arizona was where he dreamed of spending his first post-war vacation. Before long, Eriksson told me, his sleuthing established that Greenacre was well thought of, and one evening, after the carpenters had finished eating, he invited Greenacre to take a walk with him. Even though the two were alone, Eriksson remained cautious, revealing nothing about Mao's murder. He did, however, speak of her abduction and rape, and that, it turned out, was quite enough to make Greenacre propose that he and Eriksson walk over to the chaplain's quarters immediately. On the way, Greenacre told Eriksson that the chaplain, Captain Gerald Kirk, came from Ogden, Utah; he was a Mormon, Eriksson learned, and so was Greenacre.

Mrs. Eriksson, who was once more plying her husband and me with coffee and cake, put in, "Sven and I are Lutherans. In our part of Minnesota, just about everyone is."

It was ten at night when Eriksson sat down to talk with Kirk, and he found he was able to speak more freely than he had even to Curly Rowan. Eriksson remembers having a deep feeling of ease and calm, as though he were at long last ceasing to be a fugitive from injustice. Greenacre was present throughout the talk, at Eriksson's insistence. "Boyd had been a big help," he told me. "I hadn't let out anything to him about the murder, but as long as I was with Chaplain Kirk, I thought he was entitled to hear everything." The gesture impressed him, the chaplain has since told me. "With Greenacre there, it meant that Sven was waiving his right to my silence," he said. Impressed though he may have been, he heard Eriksson out with some skepticism, for before Kirk entered the Mormon priesthood he had spent ten years as a policeman on the Salt Lake City force. "I listened to Sven's story with a cop's ear," the chaplain said. "I wanted to be very sure that he himself hadn't taken part in the rape. Coming to me, the way he did, he might have been trying to save his neck by turning state's evidence, so to speak." Kirk therefore interrupted Eriksson frequently, challenging him to tie together details that at first seemed contradictory. Gradually, though, the cop's ear gave way to the chaplain's. "I decided I was hearing an individual who wished he could have saved that girl but hadn't been able to," Kirk told me. "I can assure you he wasn't being paranoid in thinking he might be shot in the back for seeing me. In war—at least, the war we were in—it was nothing unusual to hear shots that were unexplained, to find a body that might or might not have been shot in combat. Where we were, it was a time and place for thousands of men to play for keeps, and that certainly included Meserve and the others in the patrol, because if they wanted to eliminate Sven as a potential witness they had the M-16s to do it with."

Eriksson finished telling his story to the chaplain toward midnight, whereupon Kirk pressed him closely, as Vorst had done earlier, to determine whether he was certain in his mind that he was prepared to endure not just the cross-examinations but the risks attendant upon appearing as a government witness in open court. When Eriksson reaffirmed that he was, Kirk picked up his phone and called the Criminal Investigation Division office at Camp Radcliff. "I'd never known the Army had any such unit," Eriksson told me. In ten minutes, a pair of agents entered the chaplain's quarters, and Eriksson, as his affidavit shows, told them, in a signal example of understatement, "This [the rape and murder] has been bothering me since it happened, and I went to the chaplain tonight and told him what had happened." The agents interrogated him with a cool, neutral competence. "They weren't shocked, or anything like that," Eriksson recalls. "They were just doing their job." Once the pair had assessed the gravity of the crimes being charged, they moved swiftly. "The next thing I knew, I was in jail," Eriksson told me. "They locked me up in a steel box, in solitary. For protective custody, they said."

FROM that point on, Eriksson's life in the Army was radically changed. Released from jail in a few hours, he found himself no longer a lone, underground accuser but, instead, a cog in an elaborate law-enforcement machine, whose purpose was to gather evidence, question suspects, and generally determine whether "a case" existed. Once the investigation of Mao's murder had been set in motion, Eriksson was frequently consulted by a variety of experts, among them pathologists, C.I.D. agents, lawyers, and ballistics and firearms specialists. Even his routine duties as a G.I. now had to do with law enforcement, for he was reassigned to the 545th Military Police Company at Camp Radcliff, in which outfit he guarded high-ranking officers, pulled gate duty, made periodic "sweeps" of the base area for signs of infiltrating V.C., and, every day at 4 P.M., climbed into "the drunk wagon," which was an M.P. bus that collected G.I.s who had fallen on hard times in "Sin City," a section of bars and bordellos in An Khe, two miles away. "The C.I.D. wouldn't let me become a door gunner," Eriksson told me. "They put a hold on my transfer forms. They said that door-gunner duty was too dangerous—that if I was going to be any use as a witness I had to stay alive."

Eriksson recognized the abrupt transformation of his military life the morning after his meeting with Kirk. Almost before he was awake, M.P.s escorted him from his cell to the Provost Marshal's office, where he underwent a further interrogation. "Technically, I myself was a suspect," Eriksson told me. "The C.I.D. carefully explained that to me, informing me of my legal rights, one of which was to shut up." When the interrogation was over, he was asked to lead a search party to the spot on Hill 192 where he had claimed that Mao's body could be found. Accompanied by a squad of armed enlisted men, as a precaution against an enemy ambush, the search party set out early the following morning, December 9th, flying from An Khe to an airstrip near Captain Vorst's company headquarters. In charge of the group were a colonel, a major, and, after they reached the airstrip, Captain Vorst himself, who maintained silence toward Eriksson. Among its members were C.I.D. agents, photographers, a firearms expert, and a ballistics man. The group walked from the airstrip to Hill 192. It was a six-hour trek, over difficult terrain, and when the men finally stood just below the summit, several of them, who were unaccustomed to tramping so long, were near exhaustion. Eriksson himself stood scanning the landscape intently, looking for the curiously shaped rock formation where the stabbed girl had been shot. Eriksson had considered the jutting and twisted rock a highly unusual one, but now, refamiliarizing himself with his surroundings, he saw, to his surprise, that it had a practically identical twin close by. It had to be on one of the two rocks that the girl lay, Eriksson knew, and to spare the others in the party unnecessary exertion he screened out the nearer rock by himself, doggedly plunging through formidable brush to reach it. Mao wasn't there, and Eriksson, rejoining the waiting group, pointed to the other rock. "That's where she is," he said, with certainty. After the others fell in behind him, he walked silently to the second rock, seventy-five metres away. In due course, they came upon Mao, her remains a rigid crescent settled grotesquely in a half nest of soil and rocks and matted foliage. She had lain moldering there for three weeks and her body was badly decayed. As the others clustered around it, Eriksson withdrew to the fringes of the circle, made uncomfortable by everyone's purposeful curiosity. "It was another case of people doing their job," he told me. "They hadn't ever heard Mao's voice or seen her carrying Manuel's pack."

Going about their tasks with unrelieved efficiency, the men staked out an area thirty feet square in which to conduct their operations, soon gathering a harvest of clues, among them lead fragments of spent bullets, for the ballistics and firearms men, and parts of Mao's remains, for the pathologists. The corpse itself was placed in an Army "casualty bag" —a rubberized olive-drab shroud, originally designed for fallen soldiers. There was to be an autopsy at the United States Army mortuary in Saigon, by a Japanese anthropologist, Professor Tadao Furue, of Tokyo University, and Colonel Pierre A. Finck, commanding officer of the 9th Medical Laboratory. (Dr. Finck, a well-known Army pathologist, was one of the team of three physicians that performed the autopsy on the late President Kennedy.) Throughout, Eriksson recalls, dozens of pictures were taken, for possible use as trial exhibits, the flashes of the photographers' bulbs pale in the afternoon sun. Additional pictures were taken a week later, when Eriksson led a second pilgrimage to Hill 192. The search party was a smaller one this time, Eriksson said, its assignment to make certain that nothing of any conceivable courtroom value still lay hidden in the area around Mao's body; eventually, a C.I.D. agent, poking through leaves with a bayonet, found teeth, finger bones, and yet more bullet fragments, all of which he deposited in a plastic bag.

The evidence gained as a result of the two field trips played an important part in the judicial proceedings, Eriksson told me. For example, the ballistics and firearms specialists, working together, were able to analyze the lead bullet fragments as having come from an M-16 rifle and to offer it as their judgment in court that Mao had been shot at close range—a judgment that afforded a presumably objective basis for incriminating Clark, at least, as one of her assassins. Professor Furue and Colonel Finck also appeared as witnesses, to offer information based on clinical studies they had made of Mao's skeletal parts in Saigon. The experts' findings established conclusively that Mao had been stabbed three times, in the rib cage and the neck, and that her skull presented a "crushed" appearance, "showing the shattering effects of two high-velocity-missile wounds." Classifying her "racial stock" as Mongoloid, Professor Furue placed Mao's age at between eighteen and twenty and her height at five feet four and a half inches—somewhat greater than Eriksson had estimated it to be in talking with me. A veteran of thirty-five thousand autopsies, Professor Furue told the court, "Compared with other female Mongoloids, Mao's remains were well developed, a well-balanced body build."

Meserve, Clark, and the two Diazes were taken into custody the day after the first search party made its visit to Hill 192. Arrested by military policemen at scattered points, the four soldiers passed through Vorst's area in the late afternoon and saw the Captain briefly. His farewell to them was succinct. Recalling it for investigators later on, Manuel stated, "He told us he had attempted to keep the incident quiet but that now he couldn't give us any further advice or help." The M.P.s took the enlisted men to the Provost Marshal's office at An Khe, where they were given an initial interrogation before being remanded to the stockade at Long Binh. It didn't take many further interrogations to convince the law-enforcement officers that they had "a case," for Rafe and Manuel readily signed affidavits whose substance supported Eriksson's account of "the incident on Hill 192"—the name by which Mao's murder became known among the military. (Asked by a C.I.D. man, "Who raped or had sexual intercourse with the girl?," Manuel replied, "Sergeant Meserve, Clark, R. Diaz, and myself. Eriksson did not have sexual intercourse or harm her in any way.") Meserve and Clark denied any wrongdoing, and the leader of the misbegotten patrol insisted that his motives had been misconstrued. He had only been fooling, he testified, when he talked of having "fun" on

the reconnaissance mission. As he recalled his briefing, he had told the men, "It'd be nice if we could
pick up five women for the five days up there and
have an orgy," and then, he said, "everybody had
made comments and laughed." As for going to
Mao's hamlet, the Sergeant said that he had led the
patrol there to look for V.C., and that he had captured the girl because she had behaved suspiciously
inside her hootch. When Meserve ended his testimony, the prosecutor inquired how many times and
to whom he had "told the story you just told on the
witness stand."

"Numerous times, sir," the Sergeant replied.
"Mostly to my lawyer."

THE four courts-martial took place in the winter of
1967, within a period of about ten days in the middle of March. The trials were held in a courthouse
at Camp Radcliff, a frame structure measuring
thirty feet by thirty and roofed with tin. The weather
had turned hot and dry, Eriksson remembers, and
the interior of the courtroom throbbed with the
whirr of electric fans. Outside, a diesel generator,
the base camp's source of electricity, made a con-

stant racket, causing the law officers frequently to request witnesses to raise their voices. The participants in the cases, including lawyers, witnesses, law officers, and members of the court, lived in tents near the courthouse, and often at night the vicious thump of artillery shells, enemybound, from the edges of the division base disturbed the quiet of the legal encampment.

Throughout each trial, Eriksson said, the exponents of military law strove diligently to apply judicial rules largely borrowed from civilian law, as though they were seeking to re-create a semblance of civilian life. Eriksson found it impressive that these procedures should be so punctiliously observed within easy artillery range of the enemy—which, he added, was not to say that he was unaware of various shortcomings. Uninitiated though he was in the ways of jurisprudence, Eriksson said, he found it odd that defense lawyers could freely engage him in conversation during court recesses, questioning him on subjects that he was later asked about under oath when the court session was resumed. And, in fact, Eriksson told me, a C.I.D. man attending the sessions assured him that this was highly improper. "But then I don't know how much the C.I.D. fellows knew about law," Eriksson said. "One of them, I know, goofed on his interrogation of Manuel—he forgot to read off one of Manuel's rights before he started asking questions." In addition, Eriksson told me, he would have appreciated it if the prosecutor —whom he looked upon as his lawyer—had tutored him slightly in how to conduct himself in court; despite his status as the Army's chief witness, Eriksson said, he took the stand practically cold. However, he acknowledged that the prosecutor did warn him, as Vorst and Kirk had previously, of the possible consequences to him and his wife of his testifying for the government. "He said for me to think that over again very carefully," Eriksson recalled. "He sounded genuinely concerned." Something else the prosecutor did was to advise him to see a psychiatrist before the trials started. The prosecutor, it appeared, counted it a safe bet that the defense attorneys would attempt to portray Eriksson as some kind of repressed nut for having failed to join in the festivities on Hill 192. To counter any such strategy, the prosecutor wanted to have on hand a statement attesting to his chief witness's mental stability. Thus, a couple of weeks before the first court-martial opened, Eriksson found himself sitting in a cubbyhole office at Camp Radcliff face to face with a stocky medical captain with an extremely close crew cut who wanted to know whether the young infantryman loved his mother and whether he heard from his wife. Recalling the interview, Eriksson said, "I'd answer a question, then he'd wait and I'd have to wait along with him, then he'd ask another question, real fast, and in I'd come with my next answer. His questions didn't take long—maybe twenty minutes—and when they were over he wrote down on a piece of paper, 'Has no speech defects, steady manner.'" Offering an evaluation of his own, Eriksson added, "He seemed like a nice guy. When he stopped asking me questions, he started talking about Meserve and the others, sort of thinking aloud what it was that came over fellows in wartime. He sounded as though the war would have to come to an end before his work could make much sense."

For Eriksson, the trials were totally unlike anything he had anticipated. He had thought of them uneasily, imagining that the act of testifying might force him to relive the macabre episode on Hill 192. No such thing happened. From his point of view, as he had indicated at the beginning of our talk, the legal consideration of the crime was a field day of fencing and distortion, of quibbling and traps. No matter how close the questioning, and no matter how detailed the testimony he gave, or heard, it all seemed related to Mao's murder in only a surface sense. "The lawyers were playing a game," he said. "To listen to them, and to the testimony that the guys in the patrol gave, Mao was probably living happily in her hamlet." As early as the opening day of Rafe's trial, which was the first one held, he realized that it was idle to consider whether the G.I.s' punishment would, or could, fit the crime. Throughout, he told me, the single belief that sustained him was that in serving as the defendants' principal accuser he was carrying out the resolve he had made as he trained his grenade launcher on the cave complex; namely, to let the world know of Mao's fate.

Enacting the role of chief government witness was not an edifying experience, Eriksson went on. Just as the prosecutor had foreseen, the defense attorneys did try to make Eriksson look odd, but that was among the milder of their insinuations. By the time he concluded his last appearance on the stand, he had been accused of lying, of cowardice, and even of Mao's murder. One of the defense lawyers hammered away at the point that Eriksson had killed the girl when, in obeying the Sergeant's command to shoot her, he fired his grenade launcher. But the assertion was a hard one to prove, for Rafe was on hand to testify that Eriksson was so situated in that feverish moment that Mao wasn't even in his line of vision. Besides, as the defense could not dispute, the jacket containing the explosive charge of a grenade launcher is made not of lead but of copper, and the search parties' experts had found only the lead of numerous bullets from an M-16 rifle littering the immediate vicinity of Mao's body.

In all four trials, the court records show, defense lawyers made a studied effort to depict Eriksson as less than lion-hearted, presumably on the theory that proving him to be craven would automatically exonerate their clients. "Are you afraid of Sergeant Meserve?" Eriksson was asked at one point, and he replied, "That's affirmative, sir. . . . I am not afraid of him if he has no weapons." Eriksson answered, "That is negative, sir," when a defense counsel, taking up the pre-Hill 192 patrol in which half of Eriksson's squad had been wounded, inquired, "Isn't it true, Eriksson, that you allowed the squad to walk into the ambush area without warning, because you were hiding in the bushes?"

Undeterred by Eriksson's denial, the lawyer persevered with his line of questioning.

Q: How did you react to this particular ambush, Eriksson? Did you fire your weapon?

A: I was in the rear of the column, and didn't have a chance.

Q: Were you afraid?

A: No, sir.

Q: You were not afraid?

A: No, sir.

Q: Isn't it true you were so afraid you could hardly move?

A: No, sir.

Q: You think your fear was apparent to anyone else?

A: No, sir.

Another defense attorney repeatedly taxed Eriksson with having "fabricated" his charges against Meserve and the others in order to escape further assignments to hazardous infantry missions. When Eriksson was able to state that he had put in for door gunner aboard helicopters, which could hardly be considered safe duty, the lawyer persisted in reminding him that "you testified you wanted to get out of the platoon."

Eriksson agreed. "I wanted to get out of the platoon," he stated. "I wanted to get out of the whole company, because I could not see staying in a company that would do anything such as here. I realize that we are over here fighting a war, but to go out and kill an innocent person has nothing to do with the war."

Accused of shrewdness in seeking to evade infantry duty, Eriksson found himself also accused of a lack of shrewdness in failing to let Mao escape when he was alone with her in the hootch. He was asked, "Couldn't you have thought up a story [for Meserve] to the effect that you heard some noises or heard some V.C. and went out to check, and she got away from you, right out of the hootch?"

"No, sir," Eriksson replied.

"You traded the girl's life for your well-being," he was told.

At times, Eriksson displayed a certain poise on the stand. Asked whether Meserve might not have been searching the hootches of Mao's hamlet for the strictly military purpose of finding "strange faces," he answered, "I wouldn't say this, sir. They were all strange faces." Asked whether Mao's continued presence on Hill 192 might not ultimately have "endangered the lives of the members of the patrol," Eriksson said, "Sir, this girl wasn't supposed to be on this patrol."

Before Eriksson was through, even his possession of a sense of humor became an issue. This arose when a defense witness, a sergeant in the platoon, said that Eriksson had none. "He didn't laugh and joke as much as the other guys did; he was much quieter," the sergeant said.

Cross-examining, the prosecutor asked, "When you say he didn't have a sense of humor, you mean he wasn't a jokester, running around making or seeing the funny side of everything?"

A: Yes, sir.

Q: Did he endeavor to actively join in with the free-time activity of the rest of the people, or did he have to be coaxed . . . or did he just refuse at all times?

A: Oh, no, sir, it was not that he was disliked in any way. It was just that he was less than average as far as being one of the guys, should we say? He was just more serious-minded.

Mao's sister, Phan Thi Loc, appeared as a prosecution witness, her very presence irrefutable evidence that Mao was not in fact living happily in her hamlet. Through an interpreter, Loc related that after the patrol finished with their hamlet, she and her mother had searched desperately for Mao. Accompanied by troops of the South Vietnamese government, the two women had eventually come to the hootch on Hill 192, where they had found Mao's brassiere, flecked with blood; the troops had burned down the hootch. Loc's mother was now missing. The Vietcong, Loc said, had abducted her, accusing her of having led South Vietnamese forces to a V.C. munitions cache on Hill 192. Loc and her father had moved from their native hamlet; they now lived in a village several miles from there.

Though Eriksson testified at greater length than anyone else, most of the witnesses who appeared in the close, noisy courtroom spoke in support of the defendants, extolling their gallantry, their sense of duty, and their other soldierly virtues. With few exceptions, these witnesses had fought alongside the defendants, and it was a powerful camaraderie they shared, forged, as it was, in combat, where they had all saved each other's lives more than once. Recurrently, the court records show, witnesses found it deplorable that the defendants should have to fight for their survival in a prisoner's dock when they might be far better employed doing that on the battlefield; in their every utterance these witnesses reflected the view that losing soldiers of Meserve's calibre could result only in gaining a stronger enemy.

Perhaps because Meserve had been the leader of the four accused, he came in for particularly heavy praise. In a sample encomium, Lieutenant Reilly declared that the Sergeant's "character and reputation are the best I have seen, and [he is] one of the best combat soldiers I have known." Reilly also called him "a fine soldier," and went on to say, "He never failed to accomplish the mission. I give him 'max' rating as a soldier." In other connections, it was brought out that the Sergeant had not waited to be drafted, that he was currently in line for the Bronze Star, and that in the course of his overseas duty he had been awarded five medals, of varying importance, and had a conduct rating of Excellent. It was adduced that even before Meserve left for Vietnam he was regarded as an exemplary soldier, since he had been selected to march in President Johnson's inaugural parade—an honor limited to two hundred men with unblemished records. Inevitably, though, the defense witnesses were unable to confine their remarks to Meserve's service record, for—almost tactlessly, it seemed—the prosecutor would inject the topic of Mao's murder, the implications of which had less to do with the conquest of an enemy than with the requirements of an ordered civilian life. Given this confusion of values, the legalistic consideration of Mao's death sometimes bordered on the incongruous. Thus, defense lawyers raised no objections when the prosecutor asked the defendants and the defense witnesses whether a soldier who was condemned for having committed civilian homicide, such as the killing of Mao, should be kept on as a member of the armed forces—that is, should be permitted to go on committing military homicide. Needless to say, the question was not examined philosophically in the Camp Radcliff courthouse; instead, it was employed narrowly as a government gambit for stumping a witness. If he said no, he would appear to be disowning the defendants, his comrades-in-arms; if he said yes, he would in effect be telling the jury that he regarded the war as a public-works project for criminals. The trial records make it clear that the question left the witnesses uncomfortable, for their responses were reluctant and tortured. Of those who were asked the question, only Captain Vorst, "lifer" though he was, stated that if Meserve was guilty of rape and murder, then he did not care to have the Sergeant in his command.

Vorst's executive officer, by contrast, could not countenance the thought of Meserve's being cashiered. Here is the interchange between the executive officer and the prosecutor:

Q: Do you feel there is a place in the United States Army for murderers?

A: Sir, Sergeant Meserve, he joined the unit in approximately February of last year, and he served under me when I was a rifle-platoon leader, and the reason he is a sergeant today is because we put the duties of squad leader upon him—

Q: I didn't ask you for a long elaboration. I simply asked, do you think a murderer should be retained in the United States Army? Yes or no?

A: Well, no, sir, until they've—not until they serve their sentence. Then, of course, after rehabilitation—I think there's a difference, sir. . . .

Q: You would suggest some minor form of punishment, in other words?

A: Well, in general, sir, [but] in this specific case—

Q: For a murder. I'm talking about a murder. I'm not talking about any specific case.

A: Well, yes, sir, I think if someone has been found guilty of murder, they should be punished, but, knowing Meserve as an individual, I would accept him back in the unit, yes, sir.

As for the defendants themselves, only Rafe showed contrition, the most striking manifestation of which was his decision to testify against Clark. The decision was not easily arrived at, for two days before Clark's trial was to begin, and when Rafe had already been convicted, Clark approached Rafe in the stockade at Long Binh, where both were jailed, and, appealing to Rafe's conscience, told him that if he gave unfriendly testimony against his comrades, "he would have it on his mind the rest of his life." Troubled by this, Rafe sought, and heeded, the counsel of a Catholic chaplain at Camp Radcliff in resolving the dilemma of choosing between his "moral obligation," as Rafe put it to the chaplain, and "loyalty to the patrol." Summoned to the stand by Clark's lawyer, the priest said he had advised Rafe that, as opposed to defending Clark's interest, he had "a greater obligation to his wife and his child and the young woman who, supposedly, I assume, was killed, and to justice and society." The priest also said he was asking a Franciscan brother in Texas to break the news of Rafe's conviction to his wife, "to help her absorb the initial shock."

By contrast, the general demeanor of the other defendants was that of incredulity at being tried; the impression they gave was that they thought only the sheerest, most improbable sort of accident could explain their being haled before a tribunal. Their testimony indicates that they were so inured to the epidemic, occupational violence of war that they found it hard to recognize their judicial plight as a type of retribution. In the case of Manuel (the father of a three-month-old girl), this attitude of mystification became so palpable that the prosecutor finally inquired, "Do you feel you are involved in any way in this rape and murder?" To which Manuel replied "No."

Q: You feel that the government has done you a grave injustice in bringing you here today for trial?

A: No, sir, I've got nothing against the government.

Q: Well, you feel you are not involved in any way?

A: Yes, sir, I feel that way.

Q: You shouldn't be on trial?

A: Well, yes, sir.

Q: As a matter of fact, you have complained [from the stockade] that your promotion is being held up?

A: I wrote my senator. I told him I was being wrongly brought to trial.

Manuel admitted to C.I.D. investigators before the trial started that he had committed rape, but when the subject came up in the courtroom, it appeared to be Manuel's judgment that he had taken part in a reasonable enterprise, and the justification that he gave for doing so was military discipline. Confirming Eriksson's ruminations on this subject, Manuel testified that at a special ten-day camp in Vietnam where G.I.s were trained intensively to cope with combat situations "it had been knocked into our heads, practically, to obey orders and . . . they said if you were fortunate enough to get in a group where you had an old-timer who had been in Vietnam like six months longer than you had, if you followed what he said, you would live longer." Besides, Manuel testified, if he had not gone into the hootch he would have risked becoming an outcast.

Asked by the prosecutor why he thought Eriksson had stayed out of the hootch, Manuel answered, "Eriksson was different. He was brand-new. I'd been there a month or three weeks longer."

When he went on to imply that Eriksson might be "chicken," the prosecutor asked, "How come he stood up to Meserve? Do you consider yourself braver than Eriksson?"

A: I don't think I'm braver than Eriksson. I'm not going to say that, sir.

Q: Why did you want other members of the squad to think you were a rapist?

A: Better to go into the hootch, sir, and keep contentment in the squad, and keep a better— well, how can I explain it?—keep the thing running smooth. It makes for an easier mission and no problems.

Q: You don't believe the military gives a choice between rules, orders, and conscience?

A: The Army expects you to do it the Army way, and that's follow orders.

In the end, the four juries sitting at Camp Radcliff found the defendants guilty of one crime or another. All were dishonorably discharged, reduced in rank to private, and deprived of all pay, with the exception of Rafe, who was to go on receiving pay but forfeit fifty dollars monthly for eight years. All four soldiers were sentenced to hard labor at the United States Army Disciplinary Barracks, Fort Leavenworth, Kansas. There was little pattern to the verdicts, each of the juries indulging in its own vagaries. Possibly because of his coöperative attitude at the trials, Rafe was given the lightest term—eight years, for the crimes of rape and unpremeditated murder. Clark, convicted of rape and premeditated murder, was to serve for life. Manuel received a sentence of fifteen years, his punishment for rape. To Eriksson, Meserve's was the most surprising of the verdicts, for the Sergeant was found innocent of the charge of rape but guilty of unpremeditated murder, for which he was sentenced to a term of ten years. When Meserve had been convicted but not yet sentenced, he was asked by the law officer, "Is there any particular thing that you would like to tell the court?" Standing before the bench, Meserve replied, "Well, sir, I've seen a lot of killing, which it is our duty to do, because it's kill or be killed. Sometimes you hate the enemy so bad. Well, during this Operation Thayer II, which started [last October], we ran into a hootch that was burned down. Some Vietnamese people were bringing children out of . . . the bunker in the hootch. They suffered from smoke inhalation. I had to give one small child mouth-to-mouth respiration and bring her back to life. That just shows you it isn't all combat over here." Meserve's lawyer, pleading for his client immediately after this, spoke of the pressures on "twenty-year-old sergeants . . . leading men on fifty, sixty, seventy patrols," and gave it as his opinion that "this incident did not occur as the normal incident." Making his chief point, Meserve's lawyer told the court, "There's one thing that stands out about this particular offense. . . . It did not occur in the United States. Indeed, there are some that would say it did not even occur in civilization, when you are out on combat operations."

Two weeks after the trials ended, one of the court interpreters, a Vietnamese schoolteacher, with whom Eriksson had made friends, brought word to him that Mao's sister was missing. Eriksson said to me, his voice urgent, as though he had just heard the news, "Charlie kidnapped her, just as he did Mao's mother. So now it's only the father who's left—or is he? Who says we don't get along with Charlie? Between us, we've taken care of that whole family."

ERIKSSON never did become a door gunner. Since the verdicts would automatically come under review and the government might again need him as a witness, he was kept on in the post of military policeman at the division base. Fortunately, he said, his assignments involved no murder or rape cases. Only minor infractions came his way, but even such a routine chore as driving the drunk wagon down to Sin City could make him conscious of the sense of justice in himself that had been so tumultuously aroused the preceding November. It was a consciousness he could have done without, he remarked, for its effect was to remind him of Mao, and, following the trials, he was in a mood to try to forget her. "I just wanted to feel quiet," he said. He had no impulse to talk about Mao—certainly not with his fellow-policemen. To do so, he believed, might only invite their censure, enforcers of the law though they were. As it turned out, they required no invitation to talk about her—particularly in the summer months, when the torrential monsoon rains drowned all possibility of outdoor routine. In that season, Eriksson told me, when the M.P.s yakked the hours away together in their quarters, one or another of his fellow-cops would periodically recall what Eriksson had chosen to do. Invariably, Eriksson said, he found himself reproved for the deed. "But they weren't as sure about it as the guys in the platoon had been," he said. "One M.P., I remember, told me he could have understood it if I'd gone to bat for a G.I. who was murdered, but how could I do it for a Vietnamese? But he was very tolerant about it. He said it was only human to make mistakes."

Eriksson's attempt to forget Mao proved futile, as he had really known it would. In addition to the occasional remarks he heard in the police barracks, a train of other developments served to remind him of the girl. In the late spring, for instance, he learned that a change of sentence might be in the making for Clark, whose lawyer, it appeared, had asked the jurors who convicted him to approve a petition urging clemency; all but two of them had agreed, and Eriksson was given to understand that this augured an almost certain reduction in sentence. Commenting on this, Eriksson told me, "I realized that nothing definite had happened yet, but I had the feeling it was the first sign that things were going to work out the way Captain Vorst had warned me they would —I mean, that the sentences would get shorter and shorter, maybe even disappear."

Late in July, Eriksson was handed a communication from the commanding officer of his division, the 1st Cavalry (Airmobile). It turned out to be a letter of commendation. Mrs. Eriksson fetched it for me from a bureau drawer, and I read:

1: You are to be commended for the important role you played in seeing that justice was done in the recent court-martial cases involving four soldiers charged with the rape and murder of a young Vietnamese woman. Your prompt reporting of this serious incident to your superiors and subsequent testimony in court were essential elements in the apprehension and trials of the men responsible for this brutal crime.

2: The great pressures you were subject to during those critical months are appreciated. Yours was not an easy task, but you did your duty as an American soldier. You should know that the courage and steadfastness you demonstrated make me proud to have you a member of this division.

> John J. Tolson
> Major General, U.S.A.
> Commanding

Eriksson's tour of duty in Vietnam came to an end on November 28, 1967, a year after the patrol paid its visit to Mao's hamlet. He thought of her as his plane, full of singing soldiers, took off from Cam Ranh Bay and he had his last look at the unhappy land below. "She was the big thing that had happened in the war for me," he told me. His plane was a commercial airliner, the Army having chartered it for a flight to Fort Lewis, Seattle, from which point the men, all of whom were going on leave, would be on their own. Eriksson was bound for Minnesota, for a month at home before his discharge in the spring, but when his plane put down at Seattle he found that he was ten dollars short for the final leg of his journey. Fortunately, he ran into a fellow-Minnesotan at the airport, an artilleryman with whom he had gone off to Asia thirteen months earlier; the artilleryman, also homeward bound, unhesitatingly lent Eriksson the ten dollars. When the two men were aloft and sitting side by side, the artilleryman suddenly glanced at Eriksson with fresh interest and said, "Say, weren't you the guy who turned in that patrol? That was a bum rap." Smiling, Eriksson remarked to me, "We were thirty thousand feet up by then, or he might have asked for his money back."

In Minnesota, Eriksson returned to the small apartment in Minneapolis where we were sitting, his wife having maintained it while he was gone. During his month's leave, he was always with her and with relatives and friends and, in a way, Eriksson said, with Mao. Mao seemed to figure constantly in his thoughts, he said, which were concerned mostly with how he would earn his livelihood after he left the Army, the following April. The ideas that came to him, he said, had less to do with jobs than they had to do with life, and he attributed this to the incident on Hill 192. Sounding as though he felt he would be years mining its lessons, he told me, "I decided that whatever jobs I'd get, they weren't going to be as important to me as the way I lived. That had to have some purpose. If it didn't, then coming back from that patrol meant nothing."

Recalling her husband's arrival, Mrs. Eriksson said that when she went out to the airport to meet him, she could tell at once that there was a stronger kindness in him than when he had left. "The girl was very much with us when Sven came home that day, and maybe she always will be," Mrs. Eriksson said. "We'd had to support each other in a new way after she was killed. I made sure I wrote to him every day, and in each letter I put a packet of Kool-Aid, so that at least his water would be tasty. He was upset and frustrated—it was in all his letters. He had no one to talk to over there. Of course, I never bring up the girl now, because I know how much she's still on his mind, but Sven brings her up, and usually when I don't expect it." Eriksson and his wife spent Christmas of 1967 with members of their families in the small farm town up north that they both came from, and while they were there, an uncle of Eriksson's asked him about Mao. Eriksson was fond of his uncle, Mrs. Eriksson said, but, reluctantly, he answered, "I'm afraid I don't want to talk about her."

When Eriksson's leave was over, he finished out his two-year hitch at Fort Carson, Colorado, where many of the men were either completing their service, like him, or departing for war. Eriksson continued as an M.P., his duties generally less onerous than they had been in Vietnam, and his existence certainly more relaxed, since, as he observed to me, he was waking up every morning not only in his own country but in the presence of the Rockies. Besides, Eriksson said, none of the M.P.s at Fort Carson asked him about Mao—very likely, he assumed, because they didn't connect him with her. He made one particular friend at Fort Carson, a Marine captain who had seen eighteen months of combat in

Vietnam and was also about to become a civilian. Perhaps as an earnest of his friendship, Eriksson told the Marine about Mao one afternoon, and the captain was shocked to hear what had happened to her. "His reaction interested me," Eriksson said. "There had been times when I'd thought that if I had been in Vietnam longer than just a month when the incident took place I might have felt differently about it—had the same attitude, that is, as most of the fellows. But here was this Marine, who had put in much more combat service than Meserve or Clark or anyone else I'd met, and he felt exactly as I did about the crime."

Eriksson now fell into one of his silences, and I imagined he was contemplating the mystery of human character. When he spoke, however, it was about his friendship with the Marine. He told me that their bond was religion and that the interest each of them took in it had been heightened by their experiences in the war. No doubt, Eriksson said, the close brushes that he and his friend had been through had something to do with this, but in his own case he had been deeply impressed while he was overseas by what he called an upside-down mentality, which he believed explained the general unconcern there about incidents like the one he had taken part in. He said, "We all figured we might be dead in the next minute, so what difference did it make what we did? But the longer I was over there, the more I became convinced that it was the other way around that counted—that *because* we might not be around much longer, we had to take extra care how we behaved. Anyway, that's what made me believe I was interested in religion. Another man might have called it something else, but the idea was simply that we had to answer for what we did. We had to answer to something, to someone—maybe just to ourselves."

Before Eriksson saw the last of Fort Carson, he again acted as a witness for the government. That occurred in February, 1968, when Manuel was granted a retrial on the ground that although his C.I.D. interrogators had apprised him of various rights he had, among them the right to remain silent and to have a lawyer, the interrogators had neglected to mention that he was entitled to have an "appointed" lawyer, meaning one whose services would be free of charge. In fact, it would have been difficult to find any other kind in Vietnam, since the Army was dispensing such benefits all over the place. And, in practice, neither Manuel nor any of the other defendants (nor Eriksson, for that matter) paid a cent for legal services. However, a board of review in Washington, made up of three senior officers, had noticed the C.I.D.'s oversight, and it had resulted in a second chance for Manuel. ("He got a break. Another board might have found differently," a colonel in the Judge Advocate General's office told me.) As a result, Eriksson left Colorado for Fort Leavenworth, where Manuel, serving his time in the Disciplinary Barracks, was to be retried. Eriksson told me that he felt weary at the mere prospect of reappearing as a witness a year after the Radcliff trials. He felt even wearier on arriving in Kansas, when he learned that there was little point to his presence. Because of the C.I.D.'s slipup, it appeared, practically all the pretrial information obtained by the investigators could be successfully challenged in court by the defense—which meant that Manuel's confession of guilt would be inadmissible as evidence, and without that the government's case was as good as emasculated. Even the prosecutor predicted defeat, Eriksson told me, and during a short break Eriksson heard the judge remark to the court reporter that the trial was a waste of the taxpayers' money. Eriksson himself helped Manuel's case by testifying briefly as a defense witness, corroborating the fact that Manuel had refused to obey Meserve's order to kill Mao. (Eriksson had done the same for Rafe at his trial in Vietnam.) The *pro-forma* proceedings at Leavenworth took two days, at the conclusion of which the jury came in with a verdict of acquittal. Grinning, Manuel approached Eriksson, stuck out his hand, and said, "No hard feelings." Before Eriksson could say anything, Manuel turned and left the courtroom, a free man. "I couldn't tell who was supposed to have the hard feelings—Manuel or myself," Eriksson told me. "Flying back to Carson, I thought to myself, So Manuel's out. That leaves three to go."

In April, Eriksson received his honorable discharge from the Army, and in April, too, he heard of further judicial developments. In Vietnam, the jurors' petition urging clemency for Clark had been acted upon, with the result that the G.I.'s life sentence had been commuted to a sentence of twenty years. Now, six months later, Clark's case, forwarded from Vietnam, had been gone over in the United States by a board of review, which had reduced his term to eight years. At about the same time, other boards of review had dealt with Rafe's and Meserve's convictions. Rafe's sentence of eight years had been cut to four, and Meserve's ten years had been trimmed to eight. These varying decisions, it seemed, were attributable to a variety of factors, among them considerations of the defendants' character and background. Thus, it assumed pertinence that Meserve came from an impoverished home and that his father had deserted his mother, and the members of his board of review learned, further, through material furnished them by the commanding general at Fort Leavenworth, that the former sergeant had gone through the ninth grade, had no police record, was a lapsed Roman Catholic, had worked in a cannery in upstate New York, and had saved five thousand dollars while he was in the Army, and that he was confident that "even though war was a brutal business . . . he could control his aggressions in the future, like a professional prizefighter." In Clark's case, the commanding general, who was responsible for deciding whether the evidence supported Clark's conviction and whether Clark's sentence should be lowered, was informed by a staff lawyer who had interviewed Clark that the soldier in the Disciplinary Barracks was "articulate and above average in intelligence," and that, if given a chance to reënter society, he hoped to earn a college degree in either English or philosophy. It was also noted that, like Meserve, Clark was the product of an impoverished and broken home.

"As if Sven had it so easy!" Mrs. Eriksson said to me when she heard of these findings. "As if his family had any money! He was all of seven when he was driving a tractor on the farm. He was ten when his father suddenly died. Or maybe it's our winters that make Sven so different from those other men— our Januaries, when it's fifty below and the snow-drifts are so high you can't get from the house to the barn without pulling on a rope."

SINCE returning to civilian life, a year and a half ago, Eriksson has been concerned primarily with what his wife calls "sorting things out." Once he had been separated from the service at Fort Carson, he came back to Minneapolis determined to find employment at something other than carpentry. Much as he loved it, he told me, it was what he had been working at before he was drafted, and, as is often true of new war veterans, he felt restless and in need of a change. The idea that came most easily to his mind was to continue in police work, in which he had been engaged since his days at Camp Radcliff, but on applying to the State Highway Patrol for a post as motorcycle cop he discovered that this was impracticable. "My height," Eriksson said. "I was an inch too short." Somewhat gratefully, he went back to his prewar, and well-paid, job of cabinet-making at the small department store. For a number of months, though, he found it less than exhilarating to pick up where he had left off. Everything around him, he said, impressed him as pointless and arid —his fellow-workers, the monotony of clock punching, and even, at times, his beloved carpentry. His discontent abated when he managed to remind himself of the plan he had made during his leave to reach out beyond his jobs, whatever they might be. Acting on this, he enrolled in a non-credit course at the University of Minnesota designed to teach adults with an inadequate education how to study.

Speaking matter-of-factly, Mrs. Eriksson said, "Out in the boonies, where we come from, you get an A if you don't throw erasers."

His interest in religion still strong, Eriksson took part in church activities, he told me; he had recently supervised a group of high-school-age boys and girls making a two-week retreat on an island in a lake between Minnesota and Canada.

"Sven wasn't raised churchy," Mrs. Eriksson remarked. "His parents stayed home plenty of Sundays."

Eriksson expects that such steps as he has taken will be succeeded in time by others, though he has no idea at the moment what these may be. He hopes to open a small carpentry shop of his own in several years, but, ideally, he would like to be a farmer—a career that he doubts he will ever be able to afford. He has yet to come to terms with the incident on Hill 192, Eriksson told me. He still has a tendency to fight off its memory, he said, and he thinks the reason for this is that although the experience he had may have revealed certain strengths in himself, he is far more concerned with the limitations it exposed. The thought of them, he said, makes him feel discouraged at times about his future, which, he pointed out, could be a long one. "I'm still young," he said, and it took me a moment's effort to recall the fact of his youth, and the youth of Meserve and the rest of the patrol. Eriksson was confident, though, he told me, that the older he grew, the more accepting he would be of his memory. "Things will get sorted out," he said.

Rafe's case, I learned, had taken a fresh turn in recent weeks. Last winter, members of the Military Appeals Court—the military's highest appellate body—had decided that the admissions Rafe made in Vietnam were "tainted;" that is, like Manuel, he had made a confession without being fully informed of his rights. The judges had ordered that the incarcerated Rafe be given a new trial, which, like Manuel's, was held at Fort Leavenworth. Eriksson was not called upon to testify this time, and this was a vast relief, he told me, not only because he was eager to get on with his civilian life but because it looked to him as though Rafe's rehearing would be a duplication of Manuel's second trial; that is, with Rafe's "tainted" admissions thrown out, the government's arguments would be undermined and a verdict of acquittal brought in. To Eriksson's surprise, the trial, which occurred in June, 1969, resulted in Rafe's second conviction, an inevitable finding, in view of the fact that Rafe pleaded guilty to the charge of unpremeditated murder. Rafe received a punishment of four years' imprisonment, plus a monthly forfeiture of fifty dollars in pay. It was the same sentence he had been serving, but now, having been transformed into a new verdict, it was subject to another review, the effects of which soon worked to Rafe's advantage, for in August, 1969, the commanding general at Fort Leavenworth shortened his term to twenty-two months. The G.I. already had more prison time than that to his credit, so the force of the general's ruling was to bring about Rafe's immediate release from confinement. He is now on duty as a soldier in the United States while awaiting further word on his case, which since September has been in the hands of a board of review. Inasmuch as the board may only affirm or reduce Rafe's sentence, any changes that it makes will necessarily fall under the heading of good news for him; for example, the board may decide that Rafe served too long a sentence by five or six months, in which event it will be incumbent upon the Army to restore back pay for that period; it is also within the board's power to reverse Rafe's dishonorable discharge.

Eriksson told me he has no qualms about Rafe's being at large, because Rafe's remorse over the criminal episode had been evident to everybody in the Radcliff courtroom. Eriksson conceded, however, that the prospect of Meserve's and Clark's freedom did disturb him. As far as he knew, he said, no legal developments were brewing in their behalf—not that it made much difference, he added, since he had learned just a few weeks earlier that Meserve and Clark stood to be declared eligible for parole before they had served even half their time at Fort Leavenworth. "They may be out in a few months," he said. "It will even be possible for them to join the Army again."

"Sven had to do what he did," Mrs. Eriksson said. "If he'd kept quiet, he would have been impossible to live with."

Regardless of when Meserve and Clark get out, Eriksson thinks, the atmosphere of civilian life may exert a moderating influence on their outlook. He has no idea to what extent that may operate, however; nor is he prepared, he said, to bank on anything so abstract. "Kirsten and I have talked about the day of their release," he told me, "and our realistic hope is that Meserve and Clark have been able to see for themselves what they've done."

"What else can we hope?" Mrs. Eriksson asked. "We would be fools to think those men couldn't do again what they did before."

He would never cease to condemn the members of

the patrol personally for their crime, Eriksson said, but that didn't mean they were beyond pity. Other soldiers, he said, might just as easily have betrayed the weakness that the four men had betrayed on Hill 192, but it had fallen to Meserve and Clark and Rafe and Manuel in particular to act as they had. Speaking evenly, Eriksson said, "They were among the ones—among the few—who did what everyone around them wanted to do." Nor was he himself free of blame, he went on, without pausing— once again referring to the limitations within himself that he had glimpsed in Asia. He had yet to exonerate himself from the self-imposed charge of having failed to save Mao's life. He had no idea how long this feeling would continue, but for the present, he knew, he lived with the charge daily, often wondering how Mao might have fared in a time of peace. Six months ago, he said, he had taken a Minneapolis bus home from work and, being very tired, had dozed off. When he opened his eyes, a new passenger was sitting directly opposite him—a young Oriental woman. Still in the process of waking, and not yet thinking clearly, he said, he had transformed her into a peasant woman on her way to do a day's farming, such as he had seen many times in Vietnam; he had envisioned the passenger in a broad, peaked straw hat and black pajamas, carrying the traditional stick across her shoulders, with baskets at either end for holding crops. "Those baskets could get awfully heavy," Eriksson recalled. "Sometimes I didn't see what kept the stick from snapping. They were hard workers, those Vietnamese women, picking little bananas, shinnying up palm trees for coconuts. But on the bus the peasant woman across from me was going to work in paddy fields that were near Mao's hamlet, from which it was a nice walk downhill to a stream that flooded the rice fields. That's where the woman was going in the early morning, but it was peacetime and it wasn't necessary either for her or for the peasant women she was with to smell the bodies that were always rotting for miles around, no one knew where, when I was in the Central Highlands. The only thing these women had to do on their way to the stream was breathe pure mountain air."

ABOUT THE AUTHOR

DANIEL LANG was a prominent American author and staff member of *The New Yorker* magazine for forty years, serving as war correspondent in North Africa, Italy and France during World War II. His books include *Early Tales of the Atomic Age; The Man in the Thick Lead Suit; From Hiroshima to the Moon; An Inquiry into Enoughness: Of Bombs and Men and Staying Alive; Patriots Without Flags;* and *A Backward Look: Germans Remember.* He received a Sidney Hillman Foundation Award for *Casualties of War* and a George Polk Award for *A Backward Look.*